INKED DEVOTION

A MONTGOMERY INK: FORT COLLINS NOVEL

CARRIE ANN RYAN

INKED DEVOTION

A Montgomery Ink: Fort Collins Novel

By

Carrie Ann Ryan

Inked Devotion
A Montgomery Ink: Fort Collins Novel
By: Carrie Ann Ryan
© 2021 Carrie Ann Ryan

All content warnings are listed on the book page for this book on my website.

INKED DEVOTION

The Montgomery Ink saga from NYT Bestselling Author Carrie Ann Ryan continues with a road trip romance between two friends running from their past.

Brenna Garrett needs time to think about a major decisions, but finds herself bringing Benjamin Montgomery with her. The problem? He's her best friend's twin, so there's no escaping that familiar face.

Benjamin didn't want to leave his family in a lurch, but Brenna isn't the only one who needs a break. Only a drunken mistake leads to a night of passion with unintended consequences.

When it turns out they can't walk away, they'll have to make a choice: remain just friends or start something new and possibly risk everything.

Including themselves.

PRAISE FOR CARRIE ANN RYAN

"Count on Carrie Ann Ryan for emotional, sexy, character driven stories that capture your heart!" – Carly Phillips, NY Times bestselling author

"Carrie Ann Ryan's romances are my newest addiction! The emotion in her books captures me from the very beginning. The hope and healing hold me close until the end. These love stories will simply sweep you away." ~ NYT Bestselling Author Deveny Perry

"Carrie Ann Ryan writes the perfect balance of sweet and heat ensuring every story feeds the soul." - Audrey Carlan, #1 New York Times Bestselling Author

"Carrie Ann Ryan never fails to draw readers in with passion, raw sensuality, and characters that pop off the page. Any book by Carrie Ann is an absolute treat." – New York Times Bestselling Author J. Kenner

"Carrie Ann Ryan knows how to pull your heartstrings and make your pulse pound! Her wonderful Redwood Pack series will draw you in and keep you reading long into the night. I can't wait to see what comes next with the new generation, the Talons. Keep them coming, Carrie Ann!" –Lara Adrian, New York Times bestselling author of CRAVE THE NIGHT

CHAPTER ONE

Brenna

I don't know when it happened. One day I was surrounded by family, more than my share of family, to be honest. The next, I had been adopted by the Montgomerys.

I grew up with a wonderful family. The Garretts took care of me. They loved me. They were slightly overbearing sometimes, but so were the Montgomerys, for that matter. The Garretts were funny, sweet, and loved me. My parents had helped me through college. I had paid for half, and they had paid for the other. My family and I talked weekly, sometimes daily. We had a group chat that sometimes went off so much that I had to learn how to turn off the vibrate on my phone to focus during work. My family was amazing.

And yet, I was still a Montgomery. I wasn't quite sure how it had happened, but I wasn't the only one. I looked over the barbecue area in the backyard where Lee stood, and he raised his beer at me before he leaned down to listen to what Paige and her boyfriend Colton were talking about.

Lee was another adoptee into the Montgomerys, though his family wasn't exactly like mine. However, Lee was one of my best friends, as were Beckett and Benjamin. The twin Montgomerys had taken me into their family, where I had met Annabelle and Paige and Archer, and suddenly I had such a group of friends that I was invited to Montgomery family dinners, because tonight was a family dinner. Not a party, not a barbecue, just a family dinner. With five children, each with friends of their own that had somehow become family, and spouses and significant others, the group had gotten larger.

Annabelle sat in a lawn chair, her feet on her husband's lap as he rubbed her ankles. She was pregnant and probably didn't even have ankle pain at that point, but Jacob just needed to get his hands on her, and in front of her parents, this was pretty much the only way to do it.

Beckett operated the grill, with Eliza standing next to him, rolling her eyes as he most likely was mansplaining how to use the grill. Beckett was terrific, my best friend for a reason, and the one I shared most of my secrets with, but as soon as he stood in front of a grill, he became the Neanderthal who needed to show precisely how man made fire. Of course, his father stood on the other side of him, explaining to Beckett and Eliza how to use the grill.

As Eliza had been living on her own long before she'd lost her husband, thanks to constant deployments, I knew Eliza knew how to use a grill, we all knew, but she was in love, and it was a new and sappy sweet love, so she was going to let Beckett explain to her.

And I wasn't jealous. Not with Beckett, not at all.

Okay. So I was a little jealous, but not because of Beckett. Despite what everybody in the world thought, I was not in love with Beckett Montgomery. I had never been. I'd suffered a minor crush on him that had turned into nothing, and yet everyone thought I had been pining for him. I had no idea where the rumor had started, and no matter how many times I tried to deny it, or even not talk about it so it would go away, it only intensified their knowingness of my deep love for that man.

Now that he was getting married and he and Eliza were ready to spend the rest of their lives together, hopefully that whole crush thing and unrequited love thing would die down.

Maybe.

Archer and his boyfriend were talking to Mrs. Montgomery. Marc had a scowl on his face, confusing me since the man didn't usually show emotion at the Montgomery house. I liked Archer's boyfriend, though I didn't know a lot about him.

"Why are you over here frowning at the rest of the party and not part of it?" Clay asked, as I looked over at the newest adopted person into the Montgomerys. Of course, Clay had been adopted into another set of Montgomerys before he'd even come here. Beckett's cousins had been the ones to introduce Clay to this part of the family and were why Clay was now working for Montgomery Builders.

"I'm not frowning," I said as I relaxed my face.

"Totally frowning. And I don't hear screaming, so the kids must be in the house with Benjamin?" Clay asked as he rubbed his jaw. "Hell. I had that phone call with the bank, and now I've misplaced three kids."

I knew Clay was his cousins' legal guardian, but I

didn't know the whole story behind it. I knew it was complicated and far from an easy topic, so I didn't ask. Beckett knew why, but I didn't think anyone else did. And that was fine. When Clay was ready to tell us, if he ever was, we'd be here. We all had our issues.

"Yes," I answered, shaking my head. "They wanted to look at a video game that Benjamin had over here."

Clay laughed. "Benjamin has a video game set here?"

"I do," Archer said as he walked over and put his arms around my shoulders. He kissed the top of my head, and I grinned up at him.

"Really?"

"Yes," Archer said, grinning. "One of my old sets is over here, but Benjamin keeps a few of his old games too. I guess the kids were bored out in the backyard, or just being kids," Archer said.

"Mariah is nearly five now. She is not a baby, according to her. Ryan is nearly five now, so you would think I would be used to the fact that all of these kids are getting older and we are no longer able to put them in a playpen and call it a day."

I laugh. "There's no way that you ever were that guardian just to stick them in a playpen and call it a day."

"No, and I think they'd probably just learn how to crawl out of it anyway."

"Do you want some help?" Clay shook his head as Benjamin walked out, Mariah on Benjamin's back, and Holden and Jackson laughing as Benjamin said something. Benjamin was the quiet Montgomery. He scowled more and growled more, though I always figured that his twin Beckett growled the most. That's because Beckett tended to get angrier more often.

Benjamin was a quiet angry that simmered. I called him my friend too. After all, I hung out with him as much as I did Lee these days. I didn't hang out with Beckett as much anymore, but that was because we had our issues.

My issues.

Clay went to take Mariah off of Benjamin's back, shook his head, and the little girl laughed. She started chasing Holden, who therefore chased Jackson, and Clay rubbed his temples.

Archer beamed before he followed them. Mrs. Montgomery just smiled softly as Archer's boyfriend scowled a bit and went back to his phone.

"Work?" I asked, and Marc looked taken aback for a moment that I would talk to him. Then again, I didn't speak to him often. We weren't left alone too often. Or semi-alone, since Benjamin was still walking towards us.

He lifted his chin, a strained smile on his face. "Yes, work issues. I may have to head out early, but I don't want Archer to lose this time with his family."

"That's sweet, and I'm sorry that you're having work issues."

"Comes with the job. It's fine, I'll get it taken care of, and I'll make sure that Archer gets something to eat before we have to go."

I frowned as he walked away, putting his phone to his ear, and Benjamin sighed. "What?" I asked.

"I don't think I like him. I don't know why I don't like him. That makes me feel like an asshole."

I held back a wince. "I don't like him either. I don't know if it's just because he's bad with people or an asshole. Maybe we're the assholes."

Benjamin looked at me and winked, looking so much like Beckett I was nearly taken aback. "I think we are the assholes, Brenna. Sorry."

He stuffed his hands in his pockets and rocked back on his heels. "You ready to eat?"

"Maybe. If Beckett ever finishes with the grill," I mumbled.

Benjamin snorted. "You'll notice that none of us are

over there helping. He's in his caveman phase to show his woman he knows how to deal with fire."

"That's what I was thinking," I said with a laugh.

He gave me a look as if he were steeling himself. "You okay with that?"

I held back a groan, knowing I'd have to explain everything again. "Okay with what?"

"You know, Eliza and Beckett."

"The fact that my best friend is happy and in love? What's there not to be okay about?" He opened his mouth to say something, and I held up my hand. "I'm not in love with Beckett. I never was. Eventually, I will get it skywritten by a plane, or maybe just a large banner. Or maybe a tattoo on my forehead so the rest of all of you will understand."

Benjamin just blinked before he slid his hands through his hair. "Sorry. This seems to be a touchy subject."

I rolled my eyes. "Of course, it's a touchy subject. You would feel it was touchy if everyone thought you were in love with somebody even when you weren't. He was my best friend."

"Was?"

I could have kicked myself at the slip. "He still is. Now my best friend circles include Annabelle, Paige, Lee, and even you."

"Even me," he muttered. "So glad that I'm tacked on there."

"You know what I mean. I just, I suck at this whole thing. I really should just stick to baking cakes and not dealing with words."

"Words are hard."

"Are you making fun of me?" I asked him, scowling.

"Brenna Garrett, I would never once make fun of you."

I sighed. "I still think you're making fun of me."

"I'm not. Honestly, I thought you did. I thought you loved him. Or I thought it was a crush, or it was something. I'm sorry."

I shrugged. "Don't be. There's nothing really to say about that. You weren't the only one. I had the stars in my eyes while looking at him, and maybe it was just because I liked having someone I could talk to about everything."

"You can talk to me," he said, almost absently.

I looked at him then. I wished that were true. Because I wasn't sure I could talk to anybody about what was on my mind. And it had nothing to do with Beckett Montgomery.

"You're a good man, Benjamin."

He snorted. "That's a good way to start off the

night. I'm a good man, but I'm never going to tell you my secrets."

"You don't need to know all of my secrets, Benjamin. They're scary."

"With the way that our family rolls? I'm pretty sure we all have you beat."

"And then what are your secrets?" I asked, only slightly teasing.

He shrugged. "I don't have any. I think I'm the most boring Montgomery."

"That may be true," I said deadpan.

He shoved my shoulder right when Mrs. Montgomery looked at us. "Benjamin, stop hurting that poor girl. What are you thinking?"

"Sorry, Mom." He put his arm around my shoulders and squeezed me close. "See? We're all fine."

"Yes, we are." I reached around and hugged Benjamin around his hips. "See? No violence."

"Wow, that's just what they say before the violence starts." Beckett walked in, holding a plate of meat. "Meat is ready. Dinner is served."

"You know there are side dishes and salads and drinks and other things to go with that? I swear to God, you fall in love and get engaged and suddenly are all growly and weird," Paige joked as she bounced in. "However, we do have all of the side dishes ready, so dinner is served," she bounced, clapping her hands.

Her boyfriend Colton just rolled his eyes behind her, picked her up quickly so she let out a little giggle, and he carried her against his chest onto the back patio where the table was set up.

I nearly swooned at the image of love and happiness. They had been dating around the same length as Archer and Marc had been. In the interim, Annabelle and Jacob had gotten married, and Beckett and Eliza were engaged. The two original couples were still going strong in the dating zone. Archer looked like he was comfortable where he was at with Marc, the two of them taking their time. Only I knew Paige was antsy. The fact that she had told us she was antsy was only part of it. Her family was getting married and having children, and she felt like she was being left behind.

As somebody without even a prospect of a happy ever after, I knew exactly how that felt. Only I wasn't going to be left behind, damn it. I had plans of my own. Plans that nobody else needed to know about.

I quickly took my seat between Benjamin and Lee as the two of them stuck their elbows on the tables, taking over my space. I rolled my eyes and elbowed them both in the guts, and they looked down at me.

"What?" They said at the same time.

"You both are hulking big men. I get it. You're all growling and all filled with testosterone. Stop taking over my space. This is mine. I've made a little rectangle around my part of the table with my fingertips. All mine, mine, mine, mine."

"So, tell us about how you feel about sharing," Clay joked as he looked pointedly over at the three kids staring at me.

"I share quite nicely," I replied, raising my chin to Mariah. "However, as a young girl, you should realize that when boys are so big, they don't realize how much space they take. You need to define your boundaries. Be careful about what is yours."

"Damn straight," Annabelle said, before she put her hand over her mouth. "I mean darn straight. Oh my God, I'm going to have to stop cursing when the baby comes."

Jacob chuckled into his beer.

"Maybe one step at a time. The baby's going to be a Montgomery. It's already going to be cursing out of the womb and pretty much covered in tattoos and piercings." Archer grinned as he looked over his shoulder, waiting for Marc to come back to the table.

"The baby will be a Queen," Jacob said quietly, and everyone else let out an *ooh* at the same time.

I laughed and took a sip of my water. "It seems the gauntlet has been thrown."

"No gauntlet, but the baby's a Queen. Sorry."

Annabelle smiled. "Aw, Jacob, don't worry. The Montgomerys breed true. We're still going to be there. Watching. Waiting. Montgomerys forever," she whispered, while the rest of the Montgomerys repeated it back.

I looked at Lee, who winked at me, while Colton just shook his head, looking as bewildered as usual.

"Sorry, I need to head out," Marc said as he leaned down and kissed Archer softly. "I know you just sat down for dinner, but do you want to come with me?"

There was a pleading look in his gaze, but Archer just shook his head. "It's okay. I'll get a ride home."

"I've got you," Lee said. Lee looked up at Marc, who nodded. "Seriously, Marc, he's safe with me."

There was a tiny tick in Marc's jaw, but he shrugged, kissed Archer again, said he was sorry for leaving, and left. I figured that Marc was just awkward, but maybe it was because I was usually the awkward one. Everybody dug into their food, and I looked around, wondering again how I'd become a Montgomery.

I wasn't sure why I was here anymore. Things had changed between Beckett and me, but not because he had fallen in love with Eliza. But because I had something to tell him that I had never been able to. I had tried, and he'd pushed me away because he was hiding his own secrets.

I wasn't sure how to come back from that. Things were awkward, and I hated that.

It didn't help that I would be leaving soon, just for a little bit, but my family needed me. Or at least that's what they told me.

"So, when do you head out?" Beckett asked from the other end of the table, and I looked up at him. It was odd, as I used to sit next to him, but Mrs. Montgomery had sat me over here. Was it because she thought I felt like I had lost my best friend? Because that wasn't the case. Everybody kept putting this label on me, the unrequited, sad virgin, even though I was none of those things. Nobody listened.

"I leave in two days," I answered.

"And you're driving?" Beckett said. "I still can't believe you don't like planes."

"I don't mind planes, but I want to make it a road trip. Lots of space to think."

Everybody met each other's gazes, and I knew I'd said the wrong thing.

Benjamin nudged me, cutting into the awkward

silence. "Sounds like fun. I haven't done a road trip in forever."

"They are fun. Plus, you're in control of your car. You can't just get out and stop and take in the scenery while you were in an airplane."

"No, I think if you have to pull over on the side of the air road, it might be a little dangerous," Benjamin said, and Lee groaned from the other side of me.

"Air road?"

"Hey, like I said, not good with the words," Benjamin said.

"No, I'm the one who said I'm not good with the words," I said with a laugh. "Reunion's going to be fun." I looked up at Mrs. Montgomery again. "It'll be good to see everybody again."

"And all of your sisters and brothers will be there?" she asked, and I nodded again, taking a bite of my chicken. "Yes, all of them will be there, with their spouses and the babies. And four of the women are pregnant."

Mrs. Montgomery's eyes widened. "Oh wow."

"Yes, it's going to rival a Montgomery barbecue, and that's just our side of the family."

"I always forget you have such a huge family," Annabelle put in with a smile on her face.

"Very, very much so. I think that's why I fit in here

so well, right?" I asked with a wink, and everyone smiled at me, but it felt forced.

Or maybe I just saw things.

Thankfully, the conversation shifted to something else, and we finished our meals before I decided I needed to head out. After all, I had packing to do, and I just needed to get home.

Everybody was kind as I walked to my car, Benjamin walking with me.

"You doing okay?" he asked.

I sighed. "Yes, I'm fine."

"I'll help you stem the tide of the whole awkwardness thing if you want."

I looked up at him then and frowned. "What do you mean?"

"I can see it now. The way that people are acting around you. I don't like it. So I'll help you."

"I don't need your help, Benjamin." I wondered why it irked me that he wanted to.

"I want to help you because I like you, Brenna. We're friends. Right?"

"We are."

"Then I'm going to make sure that the family stops acting so weird. I mean, we're weird daily, but I don't like the way it was just now."

Neither had I, and the fact that he'd seen it too

meant it wasn't only in my head. "Thanks, but I can figure it out on my own."

"You can, you will, but you don't have to." He kissed the top of my head, headed to his car, and I got into mine. My phone buzzed at that moment, and I looked at the readout, my heart clenching.

"Hello?"

"Hello, Brenna. I just wanted to let you know that the tests are ready, and the next set of treatments will be when you get back."

"Okay," I said. "Dr. Geller, does this mean I'm going to have to pick a donor now?" I asked with a cringe.

"Yes, a donor will be good. The fertility treatments are going well. You're doing what you should. You're taking care of yourself. Soon we'll be at the stage for implantation."

I swallowed hard. "And then a baby. I'll be able to have a baby."

I smiled as I said it, and I listened to her speak again before I hung up the phone and let out a breath.

I was going to have a baby. Maybe not in the most conventional sense, but I was ready. I was ready for my future. I did not need a relationship to make that happen. So yes, I was a Garrett. A Montgomery.

And soon, I'd make my own family.

Even if I was the only person that knew.

CHAPTER TWO

Benjamin

I dug my hands into the soil and let out a relieved breath. It had been a long morning, full of dealing with clients, paperwork, and the bank. Nothing like my typical day, and I just wanted to get my hands dirty. Yes, I had lunch later, for which I had to be clean, but my ex knew who I was and how dirty I got. The fact that I usually had dirt somewhere on my body wasn't why we were exes per se, but she knew my faults. So that meant, for now, I would stay covered in dirt and just dig.

"Hole looks about right." I leaned back, studied the bed in front of me. "Let's set her in."

We had used a shovel for the first part, but I always liked to get down and dirty and make sure that the sides of the hole for the trees we planted were set. I did that with every tree that I helped plant, every bush, every flower. I needed to feel the earth.

I may be a weird landscape architect, but it was my niche. It's what I did. The rest of my team did the same thing. I didn't know if they had just learned it from me or it was something we all did. It didn't matter. In the end, we were fucking good at our jobs.

"I'm glad that you talked her out of the Pyrus calleryana."

I snorted at Timothy and helped him place the tree. The Pyrus calleryana was famous for its unique...smell.

"Of course. It wasn't going to fit the design anyway, and considering this is right by their bedroom window? No, they don't need that smell in the mornings. Though it's still a pretty tree."

"They're gorgeous, and they smell like ass and other, um, things, when they're blooming."

I looked around the area and made sure that nobody else was around but my team.

Timothy blushed. "Sorry."

"Oh no, it's technically a construction site, you can

expect the cursing, and I curse more than you," I said with a laugh. "However, I know our client is heading around to visit us today, and so the last thing that we need is to get yelled at."

This client was a bit demanding, but I didn't mind. Their lawn and garden would look fantastic when we were done with it, but they'd had particular views on what they wanted, and while I had liked most of it and hadn't minded working with their initial plans, some of it just wasn't good for a Colorado climate, nor for the size of their lawn.

Not to mention the whole smell thing of those specific blooms.

I was excited to see how everything would look by the end of the project, and how closely it would match what was in my head. Most of the time, it matched near perfect, but sometimes things surprised me. Usually, I liked those surprises, other times not so much. However, I had to hope for good things with this one because while we were a bit closed-off in terms of what we were allowed to do because of the client's wishes, the client had great ideas and I didn't mind working with them. As long as we didn't have to deal with smelly trees.

"Didn't you say you have some big lunch or something?" Timothy asked as he frowned down at his phone.

I pulled mine out of my pocket and shrugged. "I've got an hour."

Kennedy came up to his side and raised a brow. They shook their head. "Yet look at the dirt on your knees and your hands. You're going to have to clean up before you meet with Laura." They wiggled their brows, and I sighed.

"I'm having lunch with Laura and her wife. This isn't a get-back-together thing. It's just having lunch with my ex because she said she wanted to meet me."

"I see," Kennedy said as they looked over at Timothy. Timothy just rolled his eyes.

"I don't see," Timothy added. "Then again, while I end up as friends with my exes, I don't usually go out to lunch with them and their new significant others."

"Yes, you do. You make sure you bring whoever you're currently dating at the time," Kennedy added.

"As is only just. Because while I appreciate the fact that my exes are moving on and having wonderful lives, I have to show that I too am having a wonderful life."

"If I show up to lunch without a date, it's saying I don't have a wonderful life?" I asked, deadpan.

"That's not what we're saying," Kennedy said, their

hands outstretched. "I mean, you're doing wonderful. You have us."

I looked between Kennedy and Timothy and shook my head. "That makes me feel so good about myself," I said with a laugh.

"Ouch," Timothy added.

"Well, you deserve it. Maybe. Okay, I guess I will go at least head home and change my pants." I looked down at my knees and winced. "Yeah, I should probably change."

"Don't you have a pair of pants in your truck?" Kennedy asked, frowning.

"I always have a change of clothes in my truck, but since my place is in between here and the restaurant, I'll just head over there. This is nothing," I said. "Whenever Laura and Michelle are in town, I meet with them. They're good people."

"And you're good people." Timothy wrapped his arm around Kennedy, and Kennedy just rolled their eyes. "We just love you, and we want you to be happy."

"You're starting to sound like my mother and the matchmaking schemes. My siblings are all the ones in loving and serious relationships. I'm doing just fine on my own."

"I'm pretty sure that's what they embroider on the singles' napkins."

"So what if it is? I'm allowed to be on my own. Neither of you are dating anyone."

The two gave each other looks, and I held back a chuckle. I knew that they were dating, and had been for a while, but because they worked together, they were doing their best to pretend that they weren't. I didn't mind, they did their work well, and it had been six months after all. If things got sketchy, I'd have to deal with the fallout, but I also knew that both of them treated their exes well. The two worked together, and not just at work. They fit.

I was the single one out again, but I didn't mind.

"Let's finish this up, and then I'll head home and get ready," I said, pushing thoughts of relationships out of my mind. Laura had asked to meet, and I was going to go. I didn't have a date, or even a fake date to bring, and it didn't matter. I had eaten with the two of them before, and it hadn't been a big deal. I had introduced Michelle to Laura about a year after Laura and I had broken up, and I had figured the two would hit it off. I had been in their wedding, for damn's sake. I was their friend. And even though they didn't live here anymore, I saw them any chance I could.

That didn't mean I was lonely. I was just going to be the only true single uncle in the Montgomerys, which was just fine with me.

Why was I talking to myself as if I was trying to reassure myself that I was happy being alone? I had been alone for a while, as Laura had been my last serious relationship. I didn't need anybody else. I was used to this. I was good at it. Even though I knew that my mother and probably my sisters kept looking at me, wondering when I was going to settle down. I didn't see that happening any time soon.

We finished up the job for the day, and I left Timothy and Kennedy working on the final setups that we would complete tomorrow. We had other projects scheduled for the afternoon, so I felt comfortable giving them the responsibility.

After lunch, I had a break in my schedule, which meant I had planning and meetings if I wanted, or I could take a break if I wanted. Sometimes I scheduled that for myself, and usually, I filled it with more work. I couldn't help it, I was good at what I did, and I liked it.

I headed home, took a quick shower, pulled on a new pair of jeans and a T-shirt. We weren't going to somewhere fancy, and I wanted to be comfortable. I put different boots on this time, not my stained work boots, and called that dressing up.

The café we were meeting at was only down the block from my house, so I walked, enjoying the fresh air. I worked outdoors every day, my skin a little tanner than my twin's these days since Beckett tended to work more inside buildings, since he had Clay working for him on the outside.

I turned the corner and crossed the street to where the café stood.

Laura and Michelle were already there, their heads bent low as they spoke to one another, their hands clasped together. They were on the other corner of the outside patio, one of the more private areas, where we wouldn't be overheard by people passing or even other restaurant-goers. I frowned, since that wasn't our usual table, and since there didn't seem to be a lot of people around, they must have asked for it on purpose.

From the look on Laura's face, something was wrong.

Dread coiled in my belly, and I nodded at the hostess before I pointed towards the corner. The hostess gave me a small smile, and I made my way back to the corner where Laura and Michelle were.

"Hey there," I said, my voice soft.

Laura looked up at me and smiled so brightly I knew it was fake. She stood up quickly and held out her arms. "Benjamin," she whispered, and wrapped her arms around my waist. I hugged her close and took a deep breath.

"What's wrong?"

She looked up at me then and gave out a small laugh, and Michelle shook her head. Laura pulled back and gave Michelle a look, and Michelle just sighed. "I told you he'd figure it out."

"No, you told me he'd get all stressed because we looked stressed."

"What the hell's going on, girls?" I asked, looking between them.

"Nothing's wrong. We're just nervous. We're fine. We're healthy." Laura gave Michelle a small secret smile that confused me. "We're really healthy."

"Talk to me," I said, looking between them. "Seriously."

"Take a seat. We already ordered you a Reuben."

"It scares me how much you guys know me sometimes," I said as I took a seat across from Michelle and next to Laura. The two of them held hands, and I took a sip of my water, frowning.

"Explain to me exactly what's going on." I gave them each pointed looks.

"Well, we wanted you to eat and enjoy yourself first before we had a discussion, but maybe we should just let it all out."

At that moment, the waiter came by, dropped off a club sandwich split into two, and a chef's salad divided in two between the two women, and then a Reuben and french fries in front of me.

"Can I get you anything other than water to drink, sir?" the waiter asked.

I shook my head. "This is great. The girls know me."

"We hope so," Laura muttered under her breath, and I frowned again, looking at them.

The waiter gave a slight nod, a smile on his face before he went back into the building.

"I'm afraid to eat."

"Don't. You know this is our favorite meal."

"You guys share your food like a little old couple. I love it."

"Do not call us old, Benjamin Montgomery," Laura said sweetly, even though her eyes were daggers.

I snorted and bit into a fry. "Well, you act like you've been married for fifty years."

"Sometimes it feels like it." The two of them squeezed each other's hands and looked at each other before letting out a breath.

"Talk to me."

"Okay, okay."

"Well, we have been together for a while now."

"Yes," I said, after she paused for a bit.

"Together enough that we're ready to start the next phase of our life," Michelle said, her eyes brimming with tears. I took a deep sip of my water before I set the glass down and looked between the two of them.

"You sure you're both okay?"

Laura nodded. "Yes. Just nervous." She let out a breath. "Michelle and I want a baby."

I grinned, leaning forward as happiness shot through me at the news. "Seriously? That's amazing. You guys are going to be great moms."

"I hope so," Michelle said as she looked at Laura with such love in her gaze, something twinged inside of me. Not jealousy for them, because I didn't love Laura like that, but maybe because I had never loved anyone like that. But this wasn't about me.

"I'm so happy for you guys. Hell, can I be an uncle? I want to be an uncle. I mean, I'm going to have tons of nieces and nephews, but I feel like your kid's going to need an uncle."

The two of them gave each other a look before looking at me again, and something clicked. "You're not asking me to be an uncle, are you?" I whispered.

"No," Laura said, but she rolled her shoulders back, something that she did every time that she was stressed out and needed to get it out there. "We need a donor. While we could go to a bank and get someone anonymous and have it work out perfectly, we wondered if there was a way we could have you help us.

We would love for our child to have the genes of someone that we know, love, and cherish. I know this sounds weird and odd, but it feels like you're part of our family already, and it just seems right. If it doesn't seem right at all, we can walk away and just pretend we never had this talk." She was rambling. I just blinked, the hollow sound in my head ringing.

"You want my...you want my..." my voice trailed off.

Michelle let out a breath. "We want your sperm. Sorry for laying it all out there, but we want your sperm. We realize that it's an odd question to ask, and something very deeply personal, and maybe the idea of going to a bank where it would just be random and anonymous would be better, but we want to know who's part of our family. And we already consider you part of it. I mean, you accepted me with open arms even as you introduced me to your ex. We're a peculiar bunch, and we love you."

Laura nodded. "We love you very much."

"I don't...Why me?" I asked again.

"We just told you," Laura answered with an awkward laugh. "We love you. We like you. The idea that the Montgomerys would be truly taking over the world if we increased the bunch, we feel like we want you to be part of this, in a bizarre way. And now that

I'm saying this out loud, it sounds like we're trying to be a poly-romance, and we aren't."

That made me chuckle. "Yes, we're not like that, but hell. I just, can I have time? I want to help you guys however I can, but I need time."

I couldn't think, because what the hell would this mean? I wouldn't be a father, and I would help create life, bring joy to their family, and help make a new baby. It would be clinical. It wouldn't be real. Or maybe it would, and I was thinking too hard about it. I just needed to think, but I couldn't. I wanted nothing to do with the food on my plate, and the girls looked at me and sighed.

"Of course you can have all the time in the world. The less time, the better, since we're working on fertility meds, but you have time. We're never going to pressure you into anything. And if you say no," Laura added, "That's fine. We don't have to talk about it again, and you will always be this baby's uncle. We will always be open with our child as to how things occurred. If that makes sense."

"So your child would know if I was the one who donated," I said, my voice wooden, trying to breathe.

"Yes," Michelle said. "Secrets change things, and we don't want it to be like that. If this isn't what you want, just tell us."

"No, I don't know what I want. I just need a moment to think, to breathe. I wasn't expecting this at lunch."

"And we kind of ruined your Reuben, didn't we?" Laura asked, and I chuckled.

"Maybe I'll just take it home and eat it later."

"Okay," Laura said, a wobbly smile on her face. I cursed under my breath, pushed my seat back, and stood up before I kissed the top of her head, and then did the same to Michelle.

"I love you both. And just like I said before, you both are going to be wonderful parents. I just need a minute to think about exactly how I'm going to help the situation. I need time to think, and I wasn't prepared for this."

"We expected that. We're going to give you all the time in the world because this is a big step," Michelle said.

Laura smiled. "Very big step. We're here if you want to talk about more and what plans you're thinking, and exactly what would occur. No matter what, we love you, Benjamin. We wouldn't be asking if we didn't."

I let out a shaky breath again, looked at them, and then looked down at the plate in front of me.

"We'll take it home; I'm pretty sure you're not going to want to eat that while thinking about sperm,"

Michelle said, before she laughed. "Okay, maybe we aren't going to eat it either." I laughed again, said my goodbyes, and headed home. I couldn't think clearly. I needed someone to talk to, needed to talk it out, and I didn't think it could be my family just then. They would have questions. They would have their own opinions, and while I loved my family, sometimes they were very set in their paths. They would either be all for it and ask me why I was waiting and not just donating that moment, I thought with a laugh, or they would want me to think about every single ramification of what it meant of having a child out there with my genes, but wasn't mine.

Hell, I needed to focus.

I turned the corner, about to cross a crosswalk, and saw Brenna there, reusable shopping bags in her hands and a smile on her face.

I knew what I needed to do. Even if it made no sense, but I needed to getaway. I needed to think. I wasn't going to do that with my family all around me.

"Hey there," Brenna said as she looked behind me. "Oh, you were at the café. Was it good?"

"Uh yeah, sure," I said, not answering. "Hey, I have a question."

She blinked up at me. "What is it?"

"Do you think you have room for one more on that trip of yours?"

She blinked, staring at me. "You want to come with me on a road trip to my family reunion?" Confusion filled her tone.

"When you put it like that, it sounds idiotic, but I need a moment to think. I don't have to go to the family reunion, but getting out? That sounds good."

"Is something wrong?"

I shook my head. "Nothing's wrong, but I need to just be. I don't know. I can usually just be when you're around."

Her lips softened into a smile, and I wondered exactly why I had just said that. It was the truth, but it hadn't occurred to me until the words were already out of my mouth.

"I needed time to think too, so that's why I was doing the road trip."

"Shit, then forget I said anything."

"No, I can think with you around too. So sure. Why the hell not. It's already going to be weird on a road trip by myself. I might as well bring you along and confuse everybody."

I snorted. "I'm already really fucking confused on my own."

"That sounds about right. But okay. I leave the day after tomorrow. You sure you can do this?"

I nodded. "Yes, I have time. And I was already thinking about taking some time for myself. Hell, a road trip sounds just about perfect."

"I have no idea why I'm doing this, but yes. Come on down."

"I have no idea why I asked, but thank you."

I couldn't talk to the Montgomerys. I couldn't talk to anybody, except apparently, maybe Brenna. I would have to think about what that meant later, because first I had some packing to do.

CHAPTER THREE

Brenna

I wasn't quite sure what had happened, but my lone road trip for me to sarcastically find myself on my way to my family in Virginia had turned into a road trip with my friend, the twin brother of the man that everybody thought I was in love with.

"No, my life hadn't gone insane at all."

I cringed, but I told myself that this was fine. Benjamin and I were friends. Just like I was friends with Lee and Annabelle and everybody else in our circle. This wasn't anything new to us and didn't need to be weird. Only, why did it feel weird?

It didn't help that we'd be alone in a car for a couple of days. And a night. In a hotel room. That we weren't going to be sharing, of course, but still, it was going to be interesting. I hadn't planned on this turn of events, but he had looked so lost and confused, and that wasn't Benjamin's usual MO. Benjamin was the steady one. The one who always knew what he wanted and went about doing it, even if he was completely quiet along the way. But here he was, looking like he had lost something or needed to work things out. Since I knew he never took time off, this had to be important. The idea that Benjamin needed time to think meant he truly needed it. He didn't take time for himself like that, he always took care of other people, and maybe he did himself as well, but not in any way I had seen, because he was just that self-confident, self-assured.

Now he was going on a road trip with me.

Annabelle stood in front of me, her hand on her belly, and I tried not to focus all of my attention on the motion. Not that I wasn't ecstatic that one of my best friends was having a baby. I couldn't be more pleased. I wanted to get down on my knees, kiss that belly, hug her, and tell her that I'm so excited for her, but I refrained. I didn't need her to give me a weird look. I knew that one day soon, I would be pregnant, gosh darn it. I wouldn't get those odd looks anymore. At least, that's what I hoped.

"So, he is just going with you. Out of the blue. Really?"

I sighed as I looked over the last of my provisions. Snack foods for the road, and while Benjamin had texted saying he would bring some too, I wanted to make sure that I had things that he liked as well. I knew him, after all, so this wouldn't be weird.

I kept having to tell myself that. "Yes, and because I don't mind and I have a big enough SUV to fit us both, I figured why not."

"He didn't tell you why, only that he wanted to go. With you. That's not strange to you?"

I gave Annabelle a look.

"I don't find it unusual, do you?"

Paige walked into the kitchen. "I find it a little weird, but kind of nice. So you and Benjamin?" She wrinkled her brows.

I groaned. "No, we're not going there. We are just friends. Just like I'm friends with the rest of your family. He wanted to get away, probably from his sisters who never leave him alone," I said with a laugh.

"Well, that's not very nice," Paige said, and Annabelle pouted.

I raised a brow. "Don't pout. It's bad for the baby."

"Oh, I have to try that," Paige said, grinning.

"Seriously though," Annabelle added. "He just went up to you and said, 'Hey, can I go with you on a road trip to go see your family?'"

"He wanted to leave and have time to think. I don't know why. I'm not going to pressure him into telling me, though, because sometimes it's okay if we just brood."

"And yet you got angry when Beckett wasn't telling you his secrets?" Paige asked, and then put her hands over her mouth. "I didn't say that. I'm sorry. That was rude."

I held back a wince since she'd said the words rolling around in my head. "No, it's fine. And the thing with Beckett and me has nothing to do with this." Marginally. "And it wasn't that exactly. I can't explain it."

I couldn't explain to them that I had wanted to share my deepest darkest secrets, but he had kept pushing me away, not able to listen because he had tried to hide himself. While I understood, it didn't mean I was happy about it. And it didn't make me a hypocrite for keeping secrets. I had tried to tell him numerous times, and he kept lying to me.

Now, I needed to do this on my own. Not necessarily the road trip, because I wouldn't be doing that on my own, but everything else.

"Okay, well, if you happen to find out what is wrong with Benjamin, you tell us."

I laughed as I zipped up my insulated cooler. "If I happen to find out because Benjamin trusts me enough to tell me if anything is going on? I'm not telling you. That is the code. It is what we all explained to ourselves when I became friends with the group of you."

"I don't think we wrote that down, though," Annabelle said, looking over at Paige as she bounced on our toes. "Nope. Not even a little bit. I do believe you should tell us. Because we love you and we love Benjamin, and while we both know that nothing is going to go on there because the two of you are way opposites and you would probably brood at each other enough that it just wouldn't work out, we still want to know what's up with our brother."

"That was one very long sentence," I said drily. "And thank you for thinking I'm not good enough for your brother."

"Brenna," Annabelle snapped. "You just said nothing is going on between you and Benjamin. Paige decided to prod you just a little just then, you don't have to go straight to 'we don't think you're good enough.' We think you're good enough for all of our brothers. Hell, you're good enough for Paige too, even though she's taken."

"And I'm not good enough for you?" I said with a laugh.

"I mean, I guess me too," Annabelle said, shrugging. "Only I'm taken as well. As you damn well know," she said, her hands on her stomach.

I shook my head. "Okay, go. I need to leave now so I can pick up Benjamin at his house."

"And you're just going to another state in a car without a train or a bus or a plane."

"Are we waiting for Superman to show up?" I ask drily.

"I just don't understand what's going on. A road trip with your new bestie," Paige said, and this time she was pouting.

I sighed, walked over to her, and held her hard. "Your cupcakes are on the counter. Because I bake when I'm stressed, and I'm always stressed these days, and I love you. I'm going to a family reunion, and you know I like road trips and haven't been able to take one. It's been busy at the shop, and I just want to do this. The fact that Benjamin seemed to need it as well caught me off guard, and I said yes before I thought about it, but I still would have said yes if I had. Because he needed it, that's what we do. We are there for each other." I said most of that in one breath, and the girls looked at me for a moment before they blinked as one.

"Damn straight. And I need to pee." Annabelle said, and I laughed.

"Pee and then get out because I need to go pick up Benjamin."

"Will you keep us up to date with where you are?" Paige asked as Annabelle ran to the bathroom.

"Always. There'll even be a tracker on my phone, so you can find me. It's not creepy in the least, but we were going to do it when I was going out alone where all the ax murderers can find me."

"La la la la la. I can't hear you," Paige said, putting her hands over her ears.

"For a woman who likes murder shows as much as I do, you sure don't like to think about the fact that we could be murdered at any minute."

"You're just mean." Paige reached to pick up her cupcakes. "Do you need help filling your car?"

"This is the last of it," I said, pointing to my provisions.

"Okay, I'm done. I'm done. I'm done," Annabelle said as she ran out through the hallway, rubbing her hands on her jeans. "And I didn't want to use your fresh towel, so I used my jeans to dry my hands, and now I feel weird. I love you, have fun, and we're going to be tracking you on the app."

"Don't worry, we all are. Archer has a plan."

"You guys scare me," I said, shaking my head.

"You're taking a Montgomery outside the state borders. I feel like we need to let the world know beforehand." Annabelle grinned, and that made me laugh.

"You're right. I should alert the media. The Montgomerys are invading the rest of the US, not just Colorado. It could be an end of an era."

"And the beginning of world domination," Paige said as she threw her hair back, and I shook my head before I gathered my things and followed them out the door.

I stuffed my cooler on the back seat floor and looked around my storage area as the girls drove off. There was still half of the trunk, half of the backseats, and all of the space on Benjamin's side for what he needed. And because I wasn't that much of an asshole, I would let him drive if he wanted to.

I wasn't going to force him to watch me drive the entire way, but I wasn't even sure I had ever driven with Benjamin in the car. Beckett usually drove us around, or Lee. Benjamin and I usually ended up in the passenger seat or backseat if we ever went as a group just because we were the most easygoing.

Which was an odd thing to think because I wasn't easygoing to anyone except for Beckett. I wasn't going to think about that, because it didn't matter. Beckett was happy, and I was going to be happy soon. Not that I was unhappy, but I was going to add more happiness to my repertoire. I was going to stop making things so weird.

I got in the car, checked my mirrors, made sure I had a full tank of gas and that my hybrid was charged, and made my way to Benjamin's.

My mom texted me as I pulled into his driveway, and I looked down at my phone.

Mom: *See you soon. And I can still bring the Jackson boy if you want.*

I groaned, knowing that this was only the start. It was going to be an excruciating yet fulfilling weekend.

Me: *It's a family reunion. Stop setting me up on a date.*

Mom: *It's a family reunion where we could make a new family. I'm going to invite him. I don't want the tables to be uneven.*

I groaned, my cheeks heating as I looked up, and Benjamin walked forward, he had a large duffle, a small cooler, and that was it. How the hell had he had packed so little when I seem to have packed the rest of the world?

Men.

As soon as I looked at him, the way he smiled at me, even with a little embarrassment on his gaze, I knew I would do something stupid.

Me: *I'm bringing someone—no need to invite strangers for food.*

My phone rang even as I got out of the car and opened up the back hatch. Benjamin nodded at my phone and went to the back to put his things away.

"Who are you bringing? What is his name? What does he do? How long have you been together, and when are you getting married?"

I ignored most of her questions since she was mostly joking. Mostly. "Yes, my friend Benjamin is coming with me. We're driving together."

"Benjamin? As in Beckett's Benjamin?"

"As in *my* Benjamin," I said, and Benjamin's brows winged up, and I held back a curse. "As in my *friend* Benjamin. Beckett's twin. He's coming with me on the trip."

"Oh, oh, oh, when did this happen? You're going to have to tell me everything, and I love you so much. And don't worry. We will make sure that he gets everything that he needs, and I will tell everybody that he's on his way. Now, no one needs to worry about you."

And that was the crux of it. Everybody was always worried about dear old Brenna, the last single Garrett, just like Benjamin was the last single Montgomery.

I cringed, knowing that I had put my foot in my mouth, and frankly, I had probably signed Benjamin up for far more than he had thought when he asked me if he could come.

"We're just friends, Mom."

"Oh, shush, you wouldn't be taking a friend to a family reunion across state lines if you were just friends. But don't worry. You don't have to tell me if it's something serious. You just take your time with that. I'm just so happy for you, Brenna. I love you so much, and I can't wait to meet him. Of course, I met Beckett, but he has to be different than Benjamin. Are they identical?"

"I've got to go, Mom. We're loading the car now."

"We. Because you're a *we*. Oh, I love it. I love you."

I groaned as the line went dead, and I leaned my forehead against the car. "I fucked up."

Benjamin chuckled beside me. "Let me guess. Your mom went my mom's route with being overbearing when it comes to being single."

I opened an eye and glared. "At least for a guy, it's not as bad, right?"

"As I haven't seen your mom in action, I can't tell you that. I don't think it crosses gender lines, as much as it depends on the person hemming you in."

"My mom was about to bring the neighbor boy over for me to have a date for a family reunion when I accidentally on purpose said that you were coming with me. As my friend, but you heard my mother, there may be an officiant for a wedding." I put my hands over my face and screamed, and Benjamin reached out and gripped my shoulder. I startled, looking up at him. "I'm an idiot."

"You're not an idiot. You have a mom who thinks she knows what's best for you, and I understand that. I'll play your fake boyfriend if that's what you want, though I don't think I'm going to be very good at it."

I shook my head even though my heart swelled at the thought. "I don't need you to play my fake boyfriend. You do need to go, even though we said you might not have to, you're going to have to."

"Okay. I don't mind. I think I've met your mother, haven't I?"

"Maybe? She seemingly remembers Beckett, but I don't remember her meeting Beckett at all."

Benjamin snorted. "No, that was me. I stopped by

your bakery to pick up something for Mom, and your mom was there."

"Oh yes, that was you. And she mixed you up. And I might have done that too. That's weird. I never do that."

"It's fine. You're not the first, though I guess that is the first time you ever have. I'll go. We'll be friends. We'll make sure that your mom doesn't have any secret dates for you, and then we'll come back."

"You know, you're amazing."

"You're the one that's letting me tag along on your road trip out of the blue. I think you're the amazing one."

"Then we both can be amazing and neurotic together."

"I didn't add the neurotic, but I don't mind."

I shook my head and gestured towards the SUV. "Now that you have packed your meager allowances, we should go."

"We're only going for a little over a week."

"A week means how many outfits?"

"I have enough. Don't worry."

"Well, I sure hope you do. Though, of course, I guess we could go shopping if you need it."

He shuddered as he went to the passenger seat. "Don't say shopping."

"Stereotypical much?"

"The last time I went shopping, Beckett was the one that made me try on a thousand different things even though we're the same freaking size."

I eyed him as I sat in the front seat. "I think you're a little bigger." And then I blushed as Benjamin threw his head back and laughed. "Oh God, I'm so sad that Beckett wasn't here to hear that."

"Please don't. Never say that again. Don't ever tell him I said that."

"Oh, I'm telling Lee." He pulled out his phone, and I snatched it. "No phones."

"Really? No phones for the entirety of the trip, so I don't mention the casual remark you just made?"

"Okay, we can have phones. Just don't tell him."

"I won't. I was never going to. Do you want me to drive?"

I narrowed my eyes. "Excuse me?"

"Not right now, as I got into the passenger seat, but touchy much?"

"Sorry," I mutter.

"I meant in general. You sent me the road trip plans, and we have GPSs and phones that should be good to go, but you do not have to drive the entire time if you don't want to."

"It's a long drive to Virginia."

"It's going to be a twenty-seven-hour drive? Then we're taking breaks."

"It'll be worth it. I hope."

"I don't mind. We have the week."

"A little over." I let a breath. "I guess we should go."

"I guess we should."

We started out on the road, and I told myself to calm down. There was no going back now—time to think, breathe and take a friend to a family reunion.

"Are you're letting me pay for half the gas?"

"Yes, though I have a hybrid."

"And a beautiful hybrid it is," he said, admiring it, and I beamed at him. "It's the first big thing I got after my business did well."

"It's a great car."

"Your truck is a gas guzzler," I muttered, then winced. "Sorry."

"You're right, it is, but it's what I need for work. I was thinking about getting a small sedan or something to save on gas, but I don't fit in them very well."

He shifted in the seat, and I raised a brow. "I'm not making a comment on your size again." He laughed outright, and I smiled. "This is turning out to be an okay drive."

"Glad I could help." He paused, let out a breath. "Thanks for letting me come. You never asked why I wanted to go with you," he said, after a minute or two on the highway.

"I didn't need to. You said you needed to be here, or wanted to, and I didn't mind."

"I guess I should tell you. I need to tell someone, and I can't tell my family because then they're going to have opinions, and I'm not in the mood for that."

I glanced at him and he let out a breath. "Okay then, we're not even out of the state, and yet I don't think I can keep it in."

"Are you okay?" I asked, my heart racing.

"I am. At least I hope so, considering what someone asked of me."

I settled on the cruise control, with my hands on the steering wheel and my eyes on the road, even though most of my attention was on him.

"What is it?"

"Do you remember my ex? Laura?"

I frowned and nodded as I took the next exit onto the other highway. "Yes. You were in her wedding to Michelle."

"Good memory."

I smirked. "I made the cake."

"Oh yeah, I forgot."

"It was a good cake. Buttercream frosting, lemon filling, with a cheesecake on the side, and it was so yummy. Nice and airy for one and very rich and dense on the other."

"The perfect blend of them," he said.

I smiled again. "I was always sad when you two broke up."

"I wasn't," he said.

That made me snort.

"I meant only that we weren't right for each other. She and Michelle are. However, they came to me with a request."

"What is it?" I asked, though an odd feeling spread over me, and I knew he couldn't be about to say what he was going to say. Right?

It would be too eerie.

"They want a baby. And they want the donor to be someone that they know and trust."

"They asked you!" I nearly skidded off the highway but kept my calm as a truck hit their horn beside me, and Benjamin put his hands on my knee. He looked down at his hand, let out a breath, and I swallowed. "Sorry."

"I probably shouldn't have said that while we were on the highway and you were driving."

"No. No. When else would you tell me that somebody wants your sperm? I can't believe I just said sperm. Again."

"Yes, sperm. It keeps going through my mind over and over again. I had a dream that there was a little sperm having a conversation with me about the pros and cons. It was like the devil and the angel on your shoulder, but instead, they were in my brain, and they were actual sperm. And I have no idea what's going on, and I have to stop saying the word sperm."

I snorted, my whole body shaking as I did my best not to drive us right off the highway.

"You're going to do it, aren't you?" I risked a glance over at him before I looked back at the road.

"Yeah, I am."

The astonishment in his voice surprised me. "You're good people. You don't need to sound so shocked that you want to make that decision."

"It's a big fucking decision. Part of me wanted to do it right away, but I needed time to think about it. I knew if I were around my family, they would keep pestering me until they figured out what was going on, and then they would have opinions."

"Are you not going to tell them?" I asked, frowning.

"I will. Just after the fact. That way, they can't talk me out of it."

"You know, that's probably a good idea, though I don't think they would necessarily talk you out of it."

"Maybe not intentionally, but they would bring

around different ideas and opinions even if they were on the side of doing it, it would still twist my thoughts off enough that I just...I want it to be about Laura and Michelle, not about me."

"You're a good man," I whispered.

"I hope so. I hope it works. They'd be great parents and deserve it."

He talked about them some more, and I leaned my head against the headrest as I kept driving, thinking what he was doing and why he was doing it. I wouldn't know the father of my child, but I was going to have to pick a donor soon. It wouldn't be Benjamin, but hell, what were the chances? I was never going to ask him or anybody that I knew, but he was giving another family an opportunity to build a family.

I was always going to be on his side because I needed someone to be as selfless as he was being. I knew I needed to tell somebody. Soon.

It might just have to be the man beside me.

Maybe.

CHAPTER FOUR

Benjamin

I stretched my muscles before I turned around and remade the bed. I hadn't slept too well, but I never did on hotel sheets. We stayed at a decent hotel, not a motel off the side of the road, one that might not have room service, but had doors that went to a hallway rather than the outside, and the place didn't smell of smoke, and there weren't water stains everywhere. I counted that as a win.

The fact that they had had an extra room for me at the last minute was a plus, considering that Brenna had

had her trip mapped out for a couple of months now, so her rooms had been settled. I was tacked on and might be paying the higher rate, but it was still worth it—just time to get away and to think. What was funny is it hadn't taken me much time at all to make my decision. We hadn't even left the state yet, and I knew what I was going to do.

I was going to *donate* to help two people very close to me have a baby. I didn't know what the legalities of it would be or exactly how everybody else would understand it, but Brenna understood it.

I would tell my family. Just after the fact, as I had mentioned.

Honestly, I knew that they would all support the decision. Only I hadn't wanted to deal with all of the pros and cons of it with them. Then it would be a *thing*, and knowing Paige, there would probably be a color-coded list and a planner of when I should make my *deposit* and all of that.

I shuddered, and yet couldn't help but smile. My family was fucking weird, but I loved them.

I knew that while I wasn't leaving them in a lurch because I had scheduled myself possible time off, I still hated going as quickly as I had.

I looked down at the clock, made sure it was late

enough in the morning they'd be awake, and picked up my phone.

Me: *You guys doing good there?*

Beckett: *Yep. Just getting to the site now. Clay's going to be late. One of the kids has a dentist appointment.*

Me: *An emergency one?*

Beckett: *No. Something that was on the books already. I didn't mention it to you when you said you needed time off because, hey, you never ask for time off. You and Brenna doing good?*

I didn't want to read anything into that because I knew nothing was going on between them, except for the awkwardness of whatever fight they had had. The two said that they were fine, but I didn't know anymore. After all, I had been one of the ones that had thought that Brenna had been in love with him.

Me: *We're fine. Long first day, but pretty quiet.*

I didn't go into detail as this conversation wasn't meant for texting. I would tell my twin my stories later when I needed to, but person to person. Donating sperm really wasn't discussed by text.

Beckett: *Good. Just take care of her. And yourself too. We'll be here when you get back.*

Me: *I know.*

I ignored the odd ache in my chest since I didn't usually get sentimental with the family.

Beckett: *Try not to strangle each other.*

I frowned at that but shook my head and put my phone in my back pocket. I looked around, making sure everything was packed up, and headed out of the room. I'd told Brenna I would meet her in five minutes down in the lobby. There was a complimentary continental breakfast, so I'd pick up a bagel or some fruit, as well as some coffee, and call it a morning.

I wasn't sure why Beckett thought Brenna and I would want to strangle each other. We didn't have that kind of relationship. We were friends, yes, but we didn't fight with each other. I didn't know if we hung out separately enough to make that happen. Yesterday had been nice. We had stopped for lunch to stretch our legs, and I had driven a few hours before we had stopped to get gas, and then she had taken a turn. I didn't know who was driving first today, but I didn't mind. I liked her SUV, and she was a good passenger.

She had even unwrapped gum for me so that way I wouldn't have to do it myself. We both laughed since she hadn't even realized she was doing it until she had already been doing so. It was something that her mother did for her father, and therefore all of the siblings did for each other as well.

I remembered my mother had done something similar for my father a couple of times on our road trips, and now that I thought about it, probably the rest of us too.

It was just inherent. When I had wanted something to drink or snack, Brenna had gotten it for me, just like I had done the same for her. We worked well together, and it was a good trip so far, even though I still wasn't sure why I was here or how I ended up sitting in a car with Brenna.

We had dinner last night at a local chain restaurant next to the hotel, so that way we could each have a couple of beers and then walk to our rooms. We said pleasant good nights, and we'd see each other in the morning, planned out our trip, and hadn't spoken. It hadn't been awkward or weird. It had just been... normal. There was no pressure, nothing pushing at me to be one way or the other.

I liked it.

Brenna stood in the lobby, her rolling bag next to her, as she frowned at the bagel selection. I had my duffel bag beside me and set it next to hers. She looked up at me. Her wide eyes were bright, though I didn't know if that had to do with the lighting or the fact that she might've gotten some sleep the night before. She'd piled her hair on the top of her head, little tendrils going down her neck, and it made her neck look long and inviting.

I needed a coffee if I was going to let my thoughts wander down that particular path.

She smiled at me and gestured towards the bagels. "I can't make a choice. Either way, I'm going to want cream cheese. And since I want to get on the road, that means there's going to be cream cheese in my car." She cringed, and I held back a smile.

"We'll use napkins."

"Then I was thinking about getting a banana, but I can't eat a banana while in the car if you're in it, because if we make eye contact, eating a banana with other people watching is weird."

She said everything so fast that it took me a minute for my brain to catch up, and then I barked out a laugh. Someone gave me a weird look, and I shrugged before looking back at her.

"I'm never going to be able to think about eating a banana in public again. Thank you for that."

"Oh, I'm pretty sure you thought about that before, don't even with me."

"No, I've never once thought about making eye contact with someone eating a banana. Mostly because I break it into pieces before popping it into my mouth."

"That'd probably be a smart way to do it." She waved her hand at me. "Anyway, I think I'm going with cinnamon raisin, go with something sweet."

"I'll probably just go with a wheat bagel because an everything bagel is going to make the car smell like onion and get everywhere."

She smiled at me, and I shrugged. "Thank you for taking care of my car."

"I try. However, I need coffee."

"I do too. They have the paper to-go cups, but I brought myself a traveling mug so that way I can get more." She whispered that last part, and I snorted.

I reached into my bag and showed her mine. "Same."

"We are the perfect traveling buddies." She bounced on her feet, looking happier than I had seen her in a while.

I met her gaze, and she smiled, and I held back a frown. What the hell was wrong with me? Why did that smile do things to me? I needed fucking coffee. Or I needed to get laid. Or was I supposed to be saving my sperm for later?

I should stop thinking about sperm.

"Do you need me to drive?" I asked, and she frowned a bit, and I held up my hand before I went to fill my coffee. "I mean, you can. I was just saying, if you want to begin."

"No, you're right. I was thinking if I needed to answer email or not."

"Even on your vacation?"

"As a business owner, you know we're never on vacation. How many emails did you already answer?"

"Seven and a phone call, but Paige is dealing with most of it."

"I'm glad that you have each other. You guys work well together."

We did now, but it had taken a while to get there for that, and it had taken a family fight that could have broken everything with my parents to make that happen.

"Anyway, I'm all by myself when it comes to my business. That's why I don't own an actual bakery, and I decorate cakes and cupcakes on order."

"And you do a fantastic job with it." I wasn't laying it on thick. I *loved* her baking. So much so that when she brought over samples, I had to make sure I worked hard outside to make up for it.

"Thank you. That's sweet of you. I like what I do, I like coming up with new designs, and I have my sketch-book and digital book to make that happen as well, for when we're on the road."

"Really?"

"Yes. I couldn't just leave it behind."

"I'm glad that you didn't."

"Either way, I think since you already did some

emails, you can drive, and I will work on my business stuff before I set it aside and just relax."

"Sounds like a plan."

"I'll work on your bagel if you make my coffee?" she asked as she handed me her mug.

I nodded, "Two sugars and two creams?"

"Yep. Thanks for remembering me."

"Paige is better with things like that, but I sometimes remember certain things."

"Paige is a maniac that probably has color-coded binders for each of us."

"That is true." I filled up our travel coffee mugs and we made our way past the front desk, dropping off our keys in a little box before heading to the SUV. We got situated, set up the GPS, and were on our way. It was odd that we'd already fallen into a routine considering this was the first time I'd ever been in a hotel with Brenna—even if it was in different rooms.

"We can make it tonight since it's still decently early. However, I do have a refundable hotel set up for tonight in case we can't make it."

"I remember. We're doing good."

"That way, in case we see something on the side of the road, like the largest ball of twine, we can enjoy ourselves."

"Why would we like seeing the largest ball of twine?" I asked honestly as I got on the highway.

"Because it's ingenious? Someone's hard work?"

"You're right. Somebody loves it, did a lot of work to get others to see it. If I see a large sign for it, then sure, we'll go visit the huge ball of twine."

"Sounds good to me." She sipped her coffee, grinned, and I shook my head as I took a bite of my bagel. I hadn't even realized when she set a napkin on my lap, and she blushed, removing her hand quickly.

I ignored the heat in my groin at the action.

Maybe I needed to get laid if that touch had made my dick twitch.

"Sorry, force of habit."

"I don't mind," I whispered, doing my best not to think about what her fingers had just been near. This was Brenna, for God's sake.

We were on the road for about an hour before finally she set down her phone and rolled her shoulders back. "I should probably draw just because I have the itch for it, but I also want to take a nap."

"Do whatever you need to. We've got a bit until we should pull off to get some gas."

"And then it's my turn to drive?" she asked, and I nodded, getting out of the way of a dumbass going twenty miles over the speed limit.

"My favorite part of that," Brenna said, gesturing towards the asshole driving past us, "is that sometimes we'll see them pulled over on the side of the road with a cop behind them."

"Only in a just world," I muttered.

"That is true."

We drove in peace for a few miles before she squirmed in her seat. "You haven't asked why I needed this road trip. Of course, I'm glad you're here with me, and not merely because you'll be keeping my mother off my back."

I cringed. "That's going to be interesting."

"I'll protect you."

"I thought I was the one that was supposed to protect you." I risked a glance at her and frowned when I saw her hands on her lip, tearing away at her napkin.

"I have no idea how it's going to work, but either way, I do want to thank you."

I shook my head, wondering why she was so nervous. "I should thank you."

"I'm not taking this road trip just for my family," she whispered after a moment.

Anxiety wrapped around me, but I ignored it. "What do you mean?"

"I need to tell somebody, and I haven't told anyone.

Since you told me your secret, maybe it's time I tell you mine."

I risked a glance at her, my hands gripping the steering wheel tight. "Are you okay?"

"I am. I'm such a hypocrite," she whispered, and I nearly pulled off the side of the road so I could look at her.

"What's wrong, Brenna?"

"I'm going to have a baby."

This time, I had to slow down, grateful that I didn't run us off the road. "What?"

"We really shouldn't have these conversations when the other person is driving."

"No shit. What the fuck, Brenna? I didn't even know you were dating anyone?"

"I'm not," she blurted, and I cringed.

"I'm going about this the wrong way. Congratulations?" I asked.

"Not yet. I've been getting fertility treatments because I want a baby. I don't want a relationship. Therefore I'm going about it my way. I am going to have a child. I'm going to be a mom. There's not going to be a father involved, so I'm going to look for donations. Which is why it was very ironic when you were telling me yesterday that you were going to be someone who donates."

I blinked, my mouth going dry. "Holy hell." My thoughts went in a hundred different directions, and I felt like I couldn't keep up, so I said the first thing that came to mind. "You're going to be a great mom, Brenna."

I looked over at her then, and tears were rolling down her face.

"Shit, what did I say wrong?"

"Nothing. That was just a wonderful thing to say."

My cheeks heated. "Well, you are. I see the way you are when some of my cousins bring their kids. Or even around any of the kids at various work functions. You're good with them. If this is something that you want, I'm going to support your decision. You're my friend. I hate the fact that you're going to be doing this alone because becoming a parent is a lot of work, but if this is something that you want, then fuck yeah, I'm here for you."

"Wow," she muttered, and we took the next exit, getting on another highway according to the directions from the GPS.

We were silent for long enough the awkwardness began to set in again, so I kept speaking. "So, the treatments, did they hurt?"

"They aren't fun, but I'll be okay. I'm ready for implantation or whatever the hell we're going to call it."

"I don't want to think about that, if that's okay with you," I replied quickly, and she laughed.

"You know, same here." She paused. "I still need to pick a donor."

She tapped a file on her lap.

"They're there?"

"The sperm isn't there, but their profiles are."

"I didn't think their sperm was there, and between yesterday and today, this is a lot of sperm talk."

"All of the sperm talk," she said with a laugh. "I can't make a decision. I think it's mostly I just want the baby to be healthy. I'm not looking for a rocket scientist unless they want to be a rocket scientist. There's just so much information, and yet not enough. I don't know. It's a lot."

I drove for a few minutes, thinking as she muttered to herself, tracing her finger along the edge of the files. "Why haven't you told anyone else about this? Annabelle, Paige, Beckett?"

"That's why I'm a hypocrite. I got mad at Beckett for not telling me about the shooting. For keeping his secrets, but it wasn't that..."

"You know, I wasn't thrilled with him either," I growled, thinking about the shooting that Beckett had been in and the fact that he had hidden it from everybody except Lee.

She reached out and squeezed my arm before letting go. "I was angrier that every time that I tried to tell Beckett I was excited about this new journey for me, he pushed me away because he was hiding his secrets. I wasn't sure where we went from that. Who we were supposed to be. I feel like a horrible person. He was pushing away, and I tried to tell him numerous times and he always changed the subject. And yet, did I push enough? This is a huge decision for me, and I have been keeping it to myself. Mostly because I don't want someone to say it's wrong, and what if it doesn't work? What if I can't get pregnant and then I put everybody through this situation for nothing? For nothing but heartbreak."

The clouds darkened around us as rain started to splatter against the windshield, and I turned on the windshield wipers. "Brenna, you don't have to tell us everything. You would tell us if and when it happened, though, right?"

"Well, first, I wouldn't be able to hide it, and of course. I was figuring out a way to do so, and I thought Beckett would be the person I would talk to because we talked about everything. Then it didn't work out that way, and I just needed to think. I'm glad I could tell you."

I couldn't look over at her as the rain started to pour down harder, and I frowned.

"I'm always here for you. You know that."

"I do," she whispered. "And I knew it was supposed to rain today, but I didn't know it was going to be this bad."

"Considering where we are, we're coming up on the river soon, and this is going to suck," I said.

We kept driving for a couple more hours, but finally, we hit a roadblock.

I cursed as we pulled over to the side. We saw an eighteen-wheeler had skidded off the road and hit four other cars in its path, all damaged, ambulances all around. I could barely hear my heartbeat ringing in my ears over the sound of the rain hitting the windshield, and when a deputy came over to us and tapped our windshield, I rolled down the window.

"Road's out from here on out, trees are down, and there's another eighteen-wheeler up on the highway. We're surrounded by trees here, and the only way you're going to get out is off this exit, but there's no way out of that town either. Not for now. Storm will get worse before it gets better, so you guys better find a place to stay for the rest of the afternoon and into the night."

"There's seriously no way even to go back?" I asked.

"Mudslide washed out the way to get back, so we're all stuck here. I would be pretty quick about getting that room. There are not many places around here."

I looked at Brenna, who cursed, looking down at her phone. "There's no cell service."

"I guess we better find a room."

"Damn, this is not what I was expecting."

I sighed as we pulled into the hotel, other cars pulling in as well, and Brenna hopped out. "I'm going to need to get there first, just do my best."

"Sounds good."

I pulled into a spot far away, secured all of our belongings as well as possible, and ran through the rain into the hotel lobby. Brenna was coming towards me, plastic keys in her hand, a scowl on her face. "Looks like the storm is indeed going to get worse before it gets better, and I have some bad news."

I raised a brow. "Worse than a storm blocking off the highways and people getting into accidents?"

"Okay, not the worst news, but there's only one room." She held up her keys. "We've got the second to last one, and that family with six kids needed one right behind us. Instead of getting both rooms, I only took one because I'm not a monster."

I shrugged, wondering why the situation felt weird

when it shouldn't. "That's fine with me. We're adults. We can do this."

"There's only one bed, Benjamin. The only room that they had was a king room. Tonight is going to be a very long one."

I looked at her then and knew precisely how long it was going to be. Because hell, one room? One bed?

Thank God Brenna and I were just friends, or else that would be very, very interesting.

CHAPTER FIVE

Brenna

I pressed the key against the lock, the door clicked, and I turned the handle to walk in. I could feel Benjamin behind me and did my best not to think about it too hard, because this was Benjamin. My friend. We had just spent how many hours together in the car? We could figure this out.

"I can take the floor," Benjamin said as we walked in and looked at the giant king bed in the very tiny room. I looked at the floor and cringed. "You're not sleeping on the floor. Who knows what's happened on these carpets, what little there is of it."

He sighed and looked out. "I'm sure it's not that bad," he paused. "Okay, maybe it is exactly that bad." He looked at me, cringed. "I can sleep in the car."

I laughed. "You're not sleeping in the damn car. It's cold, and it's rainy, and we're not going to waste gas to keep you warm."

"Brenna, we're both adults. We can do this." He gave the bed a tight nod as if he were a drill sergeant getting ready to train his soldiers.

"Yes, we are adults." I sighed. "Let's go find something to eat, and maybe just spend the evening stuffing our faces with nachos or something."

He snorted and shook his head as he set his duffle near the side of the bed closest to the door. I nearly rolled my eyes because I knew he had done that to protect me. Beckett, Benjamin, Lee, and I had always joked that the person that slept by the door would get murdered first, and then Lee had mentioned that the person by the window would get hit by a sniper, so there wasn't any safe space. The fact that we cared about these things just told us how tired we had been when we had had these conversations.

"I guess you want to get murdered first?" I teased.

He slid his hand through his hair. "If I have to be. Did you think I was going to let you get murdered first?"

"What if they see me first even though you're closer? You'll never know. There's no safe place."

"At least we're in a hotel with a hallway and not one against the outside world. That's more murder central."

"We need to stop watching murder shows together."

"You're the one that adds additional podcasts to the situation."

"Annabelle and Paige are far worse than me. They went to a convention about those podcasts."

"You didn't go because you had a wedding cake to bake. I remember," Benjamin teased, and I blushed before I pulled my tablet, sketch pad, and purse towards me. "Let's go get food."

"There's a Tex-Mex place across the street. We can get you those nachos."

"Tex-Mex in rural America? It's not going to be *real* Tex-Mex."

"Picky picky. We don't live in Texas. Colorado barely has real Tex-Mex."

"Shut your mouth. Colorado does just fine."

"True. I think I just got spoiled when I had those carnitas down in San Antonio."

"Of course you were spoiled, but now I want carnitas, or nachos, or just anything with salsa."

"The spicier, the better," he added.

I shook my head as we made our way out and towards the restaurant. People were still milling about in the lobby, and I felt terrible about it, but as it was, we hadn't taken two rooms, just one, and now we were going to have to deal with sleeping in the same bed together. The family with those children had a safe space for the night, and that is all I could do for now. Hopefully, the roads would be clear by the following day, and the storm would go away, and we'd be fine.

"There's a walkway over here that's partially covered, so we shouldn't get too drenched."

"Good, I'm not in the mood to be a sopping mess on my way to get those nachos."

"Now I'm craving nachos."

"Want to share a plate and then get something else and just gorge ourselves?" I asked.

"That sounds like the best idea."

That's when I noticed he also had his tablet and sketchbook with him, and I raised a brow. "You'll be working too then?"

"We have a couple of hours to kill, nowhere to go, so yes, I'll be working on a few projects, and my tablet has my book on it, so I'll figure out something. As long as we don't steal a table from everybody for too long, I'm fine with it."

"Good for me."

The place wasn't too busy, as it seemed everybody who was waiting out the storm was at the hotel and not eating yet.

"Party of two, please," Benjamin said as the hostess looked at him. She didn't spare me a look.

"Of course, you and your wife can follow me." She gave him a once-over and then headed towards a back booth.

I gave Benjamin a look, and he shrugged.

"She was just testing the waters to see if you were available," I mumbled under my breath.

"I figured that, but I'm not in the mood for random sex with a random stranger at a Tex-Mex place in the middle of nowhere."

"At least I know your boundaries," I said with a roll of my eyes.

"Thank you," Benjamin said as we got to the booth. He put his hand on the small of my back, and I raised a brow as he helped me sit down.

"My wife and I appreciate it."

I held back a roll of my eyes again as the hostess walked away, a bit sulky.

"She didn't even look to see if we had rings," I teased.

"We'll just make do."

"Okay, husband, let's see if they have nachos, now that I've talked about them enough."

He snorted, set his stuff down on one side of the table, and scooted into the booth. It was a round booth, so we were sitting pretty close together, but not necessarily so much that I could feel the heat of him.

Thank God, because tonight was going to be awkward enough.

A waiter in black pants and a black T-shirt with the restaurant's name stitched on his chest came over, a pen behind his ear and a pad of paper in his hand. "Welcome. Can I get you guys started with some margaritas?"

I looked down at my phone and shrugged. "Liquid dinner with our actual dinner?" I asked.

Benjamin shrugged. "Sounds good to me."

"That sounds great."

"Two margarita house specials coming up."

"What about your nachos?" Benjamin asked, and I held back a smile.

"We have four kinds of nachos. My favorite is the shredded chicken with the green salsa, with guacamole on the side."

My stomach grumbled, and Benjamin snorted. "That sounds like a winner."

"We'll get that set up. When you take a look at the

menu for your entrée, know that we'll be here with the best food you can get around the area."

"That sounds like a promise I can't wait to taste." I cringed as he walked away.

"That didn't even make any sense."

"Was that you trying to flirt?" Benjamin asked.

I kicked him under the table. "You're a jerk."

"Yes, totally. What can I say?"

"What can you say? You're still a jerk," I said with a laugh.

They brought our margaritas and nachos soon after, and each of us ordered a different platter that we could share. It would be far too much food for me, but I knew how much Benjamin and Beckett could eat. We were not going to have leftovers. I wasn't even sure if we had a small fridge in our hotel room.

"Now that we have service, I forgot I need to text my family and let them know we might be late."

"We put in time for sightseeing, so we won't be that late."

"We'll have to see what happens tomorrow."

"I'll text Beckett so he can let the other Montgomerys know so you don't have to deal with that."

"Well, at least they know we'll be safe, right?"

"That's the goal," I said as I sipped my margarita and texted my mom.

"Annabelle has already texted back to make sure that we're safe. We are," Benjamin said as he shook his head and set the phone down. "I told them we were eating, but the group chat is going to go insane."

My phone started buzzing, and I sighed. "It looks like I am part of the group chat now."

"You're an honorary Montgomery. You're going to be part of the family group chats."

"I sure do love your family," I said, as I took a big gulp of my margarita, feeling warm.

"I love my family too," he said, taking a bite of the nachos. "We can be a little overbearing sometimes, but it's what we do."

I smiled, feeling warm and happy and full of nachos. Our dinners came, as did our third margaritas. I was feeling a little buzzed, a little warm, and knew I should probably slow down. Neither one of us had touched our work. Instead, we talked and just enjoyed each other's company. I didn't get to see this side of Benjamin too often, the one that let himself go and laugh out loud. Every time he smiled or laughed, women would look over at him as if drawn to him, and I understood. I was the same way.

He drew your attention no matter what he did.

I thought maybe I shouldn't have another drink, but I did, because why not? There was nothing else I could do that evening. Benjamin did the same, and while I knew his tolerance was more than mine, his eyes were warm as well, and I couldn't help but wonder what would happen if we had another.

When the place began to fill up, I was full and a little drunk.

Maybe a lot drunk. I wasn't quite sure. We paid, tipped well, and slowly meandered our way over to the hotel.

"Those margaritas were a bit strong," I said, as I leaned into him.

"I've got you, Brenna," he whispered.

"Good," I whispered back. And why did all of that sound so warm and delightful?

We made our way through the lobby as people were still milling about, talking to one another, or looking as if they would be sleeping there.

Somehow we were at the hotel room door, having taken the elevator, and then we were inside and not ready to end the night.

"So now what?"

"A movie?" he asked as he picked up the remote. He then bent down and looked and picked up his cooler and opened it.

I snorted. "Are beers after tequila good? Or is it before that gets you sicker?"

"I really can't think of a rhyme right now," Benjamin said as he twisted off the cap on one beer and handed it to me.

I took a sip and sighed happily, leaning against the headboard. "You know, I haven't been drunk in a while. I think I like it."

"Me too. I've been too busy with work and just life to find time to lean back and enjoy it, you know?"

"Exactly," I said as I moved down to lean against his shoulder. He wrapped his arm around me, and I took another sip of my beer as he did his, and I figured I would fall asleep. He was so warm, and we were there on the bed, cuddling, and I wasn't quite sure how it happened, but then I was looking up at him, my gaze on his, and I swallowed hard.

"Benjamin?" I whispered.

"Hey," he whispered back.

"I really shouldn't," I said, more to myself, but I hadn't realized I'd said the words aloud until he leaned forward.

"We really shouldn't," he said, and then his lips were on mine, and he was holding the beers in his hand. He set the beers down on the table, and then he was over me, kissing me softly, his body warm and hard over mine. I groaned, unable to hold myself back as he settled between my legs, his lips on mine. I was a little too drunk to care, but not enough to forget that I could push him off if I wanted to.

I didn't. Why not? We were friends. We could do this. It would just be one night, and so I kissed him again and ran my hands up and down his back. He slid one hand up my shirt to cup my breast, and I groaned, leaning into him.

"Are you sure?" He pulled back, both of us breathing heavily.

I didn't see a single ounce of drink in his eyes just then, he was just pure Benjamin, and I nodded.

"Just tonight," I whispered.

"Okay then." And he kissed me again.

We were both too buzzed, but I didn't care. All I wanted was to kiss him. To feel him.

My shirt was off then, and his lips were on my skin, the softness nearly sending me over the edge. The scruff of his beard rasped against my nipples through my bra, and I groaned, needing more. I pulled on his shirt, and he sat up, stripping it off him, and I nearly swallowed my tongue. He was all hard lines and muscles, and I reached out to slide my fingers over the ridges of his abdomen.

"Dear God, working outside is good for you."

"I try," he whispered, and then he kissed me again before he trailed his lips down my chest. I slid off my bra, and he held my breasts together, lapping at my nipples, kissing and sucking. I squirmed on the bed as he continued his leisurely stroll down my body, and then he was kissing the top of my pants before he slid them down, and I was wearing nothing but a smile as he looked down at my pussy, and I nearly groaned.

His dark head was between my legs, and I put my hands on my breasts, playing with my nipples as he sucked at my clit, spreading me as he ate me out. I shook, my whole body on the edge of a precipice, when he speared me with two fingers, sucked on my clit, and I came. I didn't remember how it happened.

I was coming, my whole body shaking as I whispered his name, and then he was over me, and my hands were on his belt, both of us frantic in stripping him down.

The tequila was burning through me, but I wasn't drunk just then. This was all Benjamin. All need and heat and something that had been burning for too long or had come out of nowhere. I didn't know, and I didn't want to think about it. I just wanted right now.

Maybe it was just a dream, but I didn't think so.

When he freed himself from his boxer briefs, I palmed his erection, both of us groaning at the sight of my hand on his thickness. He was so wide, my fingertips didn't touch, and I pumped him once, twice, and he licked his lips.

"You keep doing that, and I'm going to fucking spill all over this pretty breast before I'm even inside you."

I sat up slightly as he knelt above me and I licked the tip of his dick, just the saltiness making me want to squeeze my thighs together even though he had me spread.

"Okay, enough of that," he growled, then he tugged on my hair and kissed me again.

He leaned over and rummaged through something, and I wanted to know why he had a condom on him, or maybe he did all the time. I didn't know, but I was just grateful because I wasn't about to have sex with him without one.

He slid the condom over his shaft and I licked my lips, then he was between my legs again, his hand working me again to make sure I was ready, and then I met his gaze as he slid deep inside. He was so big, so thick, I could barely keep up, and he was stretching me.

He took his time, sinking into me inch by inch as we both shook, sweat-slick, the smell of tequila and heat burning between us. He had his lips on mine, and then he met my gaze as he pushed in the final inches to bring him deep inside to the hilt.

"Brenna," he whispered, and then he was moving. I

wrapped my legs around his waist, arching myself thrust for thrust as we both succumbed to each other. It was too much, this was everything, and when he slid his hand over my clit again and then reached up to cup my face, kissing me hard, I came, clamping around him. It was frantic, hard, a brutal pace that left us both panting and in need, and when he came, he groaned my name deep into my neck as he shook, holding me close.

And then he fell to the side, both of us moaning, and I slept, falling deep from the drink, from him, and told myself I would deal with it in the morning. I would deal with him in the morning. I didn't want to regret this. I couldn't.

It was only a dream. Perhaps this hadn't happened.

Let my body rest, and there were no more thoughts —only him.

Only heat. Only sleep.

CHAPTER SIX

Brenna

I woke up pressed against a very naked Benjamin, his warm body hard and yet so comfortable I was afraid to get up.

Of course, that wasn't the only reason I was afraid.

My head ached, and my mouth was dry, and Benjamin's hands were on my breasts and between my legs. He wasn't even moving, his chest slightly rising in a deep sleep.

He was sleeping and touching me intimately, and he wasn't even aware of it. Something was wrong with me.

I had slept with Benjamin Montgomery. Willingly, knowingly, and I had liked it. Dear God, it had been the best sex of my life.

What was I going to say when he woke up? What time was it? Were the roads okay? And why was his hand still on my pussy?

I knew the moment that Benjamin was awake because he stilled, his body stone. Then oh so carefully, he removed his hand from between my legs, his other hand from my breast. However, his cock was still hard on my lower back, a thickness that scared the shit out of me because I could still remember the taste of it, just the barest taste before he had practically broken me.

Dear God, now I had entered my own Penthouse letter, and there was no getting out of it.

"Brenna?" he asked, his voice a growl.

I cleared my throat. "Hi." I desperately needed water. My throat ached. Everything ached.

I knew I was probably bruised, and I was going to be sore, and we were going to most likely make it to my parents' house tonight if we left early enough.

I had no idea what time it was, or if we should continue the charade, or if I should find a hole to bury myself into. That would probably be the best idea.

I had been taking hormones because of the prep with my fertility clinic, and now they were rampaging in me, freaking the fuck out. I hadn't had sex in over a year, and the first time I did was drunken sex with one of my best friends? My actual best friend's twin brother?

Dear God, what was wrong with me? Why did I keep making the worst decisions over and over again, and why did I want to do it again?

"Are you okay? We should talk."

I looked over at him then, and he was covering himself with part of the sheet, and I hated that. I wanted to see all of him, even though that would be another mistake.

I was doing very well at making these mistakes.

"Are you going to take a shower now?" I asked.

When he sighed, I did my best not to look at him too hard. Because I wanted to look at him, and that would continue to be a mistake.

"I'll be quick. Can I get you anything?"

"I'm just going to get ready to shower."

"You can go first."

"Please stop. Just...do your thing."

He gave me a look, growled something under his breath, and turned to pick up his stuff to head to the bathroom.

I put the pillow over my face and screamed into it

softly. Of course, the pillow smelled like him, and I needed to curse.

Why had I slept with him? Why did I have sex with one of the few people I should not ever think about having sex with? There's a whole list of people I shouldn't have sex with in my life, and Benjamin was near the top of that. Hell, everybody thought I was in love with his twin, but no, I had to go and fuck Benjamin instead.

What the hell was everyone going to think if they found out?

They could not find out I had slept with Benjamin. It would just make things so much more complicated for them.

Hell, for me too.

Hi, my name is Brenna, and I live in complications. That's sort of what I do.

I rolled out of bed, searched for my clothes, and pulled out an old T-shirt of mine that barely covered my ass but thought it would have to be enough for now. I got the rest of my clothes to change into once I showered because I needed to shower. My legs were sore. I vaguely remembered getting up to deal with the *after*. Well, that was good. We had used a condom. We had been safe. And that was as good as it was going to get.

Because I had slept with Benjamin.

The shower went off quickly, and I braced myself. Benjamin walked out, duffle in his hand, a towel wrapped around his waist.

It wasn't fair. His dark hair was wet and slicked back, his blue eyes vivid. Not a single cloud of hangover or regret in them.

And maybe I just wanted to see something.

What, I didn't know, and that should worry me, but all of this worried me.

Water dripped down his body, and the towel was almost too small for him. I nearly groaned as the slit went high on his thigh, showing all muscle, tan muscle.

"When did you have time to tan your thighs?" I asked, and he blushed as he looked up at me.

"I have a pool. But I still have a decent farmer's tan if you look at my arms against my legs," he said, and I looked up to see blush over his cheeks.

"Oh. I don't know. I was picturing you standing naked in the sun or something, and now I should not picture that."

He let out a chuckle, but the smile didn't reach his eyes.

"Maybe we should talk about the fact that you've seen me naked."

"Did I? Maybe I don't remember. I'm going to go quickly shower."

"Brenna."

"Shower first. Thanks for coming out so I can shower."

"Don't know why I brought the bag in any way," he muttered. "I'm not firing on all cylinders right now."

"That's the title of my memoir." I scampered into the bathroom, closed the door behind me, and caught my reflection in the mirror. My hair was tousled and looked like I had just had sex. Delicious sex. I had a hickey on my breast, and I could only see part of it with the V-neck on my T-shirt. I stripped myself down, and I saw another bite mark on my hip, another bruise that had felt so good at the time, and still did, right below my breast.

That had been the roughest and hottest sex of my life, and while I remembered every bit of it, I kind of wish I didn't. My girl parts wanted to do it again. Every other part of me knew it would be a mistake. And hell, so did my breasts. They wanted to do it again too, but every other part of me knew I shouldn't. So I wasn't going to.

I quickly showered and then spent the time to blow dry my hair after getting dressed in a decent outfit. I was going to see my mother later today, and she would know I'd had sex. She always did. However, she thought

I was dating Benjamin, so maybe she wouldn't over-think it.

I know I wasn't dating Benjamin. No, I had drunken sex with him, and now we were going to have to forget about it.

I'd never had a one-night stand in my life, and of course, my first had to be with a man I saw weekly.

After I finished doing my hair, I opened the door, realizing I was hiding from him, taking up space, and looked out to see he had made the bed, packed up everything, and had put all of my things next to my bag. He stood there, looking far too sexy as he spoke on the phone.

"Yeah, Beckett, we're safe. We're going to head to her mother's soon. Don't worry about us."

He was on the phone with his brother. And I had no idea what he had said to him.

Benjamin gave me a look and shook his head, and relief poured through me. Something must have flashed in my face, and hurt crossed his, and I felt terrible for it. I shouldn't make Benjamin feel bad, but I also knew we couldn't do this again. We couldn't.

Even if that wasn't something that would be easy for either one of us to work through.

At least for me, that was.

Benjamin hung up and gave me a look. "I didn't tell

him. Because we should talk first, and I know me telling my brother over the phone that you and I slept together in a drunken haze is probably not the best thing to do."

"You're right," I said. "I have no idea what we're going to do."

"Good, I'm not the only one. Are you ready to go?"

I shook my head. "I need to put on makeup."

"Then we can talk as you do that."

"Benjamin..." I began, and he shook head. I let out a breath. "Okay."

I added a little tinted moisturizer, some mascara, and maybe a little bronzer around the edges of my face to make it look like I had more than a few hours of sleep. Ugh, and concealer. Let's not forget the concealer.

"You know you're always so fucking beautiful. I sometimes forget that you wear makeup underneath all the flour and baking goods I usually see you in."

I paused. "I don't know how to take that."

"You don't have to take it at all. I'm letting you know I think you are beautiful."

Everything felt weird, forced. And it was all on me. "Benjamin."

"What, Brenna?" He let out a rough growl that did things to me I didn't want to think about. "We slept together. Do you regret it?"

I looked at him then and winced.

He sighed and let out a breath. "You regret it."

"I'm not saying *regret* regret, but more of we really shouldn't have done that. You know we shouldn't have done that. We're friends first."

"And everybody thinks that you're in love with my brother."

"That too," I growled. "They think I'm in love with Beckett, and now I'm doing my best to dissuade that, we all are. It's just going to complicate things. We're in the same circles. My friends are your friends. My friends are your family. Us sleeping together and having a one-night stand or whatever the hell this was will hurt everybody in the end." I didn't realize I was crying, my voice going high-pitched, until Benjamin leaned forward and wiped the tears from the cheeks.

"Don't cry," he whispered.

"It's these stupid hormones."

He raised a brow.

I waved him off. "I'm on hormones because I want to get pregnant."

"I'm glad we remembered the fucking condom," he muttered.

I swallowed hard. "You're already donating sperm to one person. I'm glad we didn't decide to make it both." I closed my eyes and groaned. "I suck at this. I don't know how to talk to humans anymore. I'm awkward as fuck. I'm weird. I'm not very social, and I get grumpy. I don't even know why I thought I could be a mom. I'm going to be like the worst parent ever because I just suck at being a human being. And here I am hurting you because I don't know how to be a human being. I'm sorry. Last night was great. Seriously. Best sex ever."

He just kept looking at me, blinking, and I kept going, knowing I might as well keep digging the hole for me to bury myself in.

"Seriously best sex ever. I'm not a virgin, not like Archer used to think for so long," I grumbled.

Benjamin snorted. "Didn't think you were a virgin. And I hope to hell you weren't, considering what we did last night."

"Drunk sex for my first time really wouldn't have been a good thing. No, I'm not a virgin. I'm not in love with your brother. Yes, you and I had sex, but we were safe, and oh my God, I can't believe that I'm having this conversation. My hormones are making me lose my mind."

Benjamin leaned forward, gripped my chin, and brushed his lips along mine. I sank into him, sighing before I pulled myself back quickly. "What the hell was that? That's not helping things."

"Made you shut up, didn't it?" he asked, laughter in his eyes.

I pushed at him slightly before I started laughing, this time the tears freely flowing. "I'm losing my mind."

"You're adding extra hormones to your system, so of course you're going to feel like you're losing your mind." He let out a breath. "Let's think about this rationally."

"I'm not rational. That's the point."

"I'm the rational brother. We all know this."

"We do," I whispered.

"We had sex. Really fucking good sex. It's not just on your end, Brenna. Best fucking sex ever. We won't do it again. We got it out of our systems, and we're going to be friends. You're my friend Brenna. I'm the last single Montgomery of my family, and you're the last single Garrett. We are going to remain who we are, even though I have seen all of your parts."

"Thanks, that's so romantic," I said as I laughed.

He winked. "Well, you've seen my part as well."

"Yes, I have," I said, drawing out the words until I put my hands over my face and screamed. "See? We can't do this." I let my hands fall. "Everyone's going to know."

"So, no secrets then."

"Am I a hypocrite? Horrible hypocrite."

"I'm so good at messing things up, and I feel like that's what I'm going to do with this."

"Then we don't mess it up. You and me? We're friends. We go to your family reunion. We make sure your family has nothing to worry about, and then we come home, and we get back to business. I will donate my sperm. You will get sperm from someone else, and I will stop saying sperm in front of you."

My lips twitched. "I don't think you can make that promise," I grumbled.

He laughed then, and the sound soothed me, even though it shouldn't—damn hormones.

"I like you, Brenna. We're going to figure this out."

"And we're not going to have sex again," I said.

He looked at me then, swallowed hard, and nodded. "Never again."

I did my best to hide the disappointment I shouldn't be feeling at all.

CHAPTER SEVEN

Benjamin

W e pulled in front of a nice-looking home with decent landscaping. Brenna let out a breath as she put the car into park and looked over at me.

"I don't want you to look at the garden in the back-yard," she blurted, and I blinked at her. Of all the things she could have said to me at that moment, and there were many things that we were not talking about and shouldn't talk about, but really should talk about, that hadn't been it.

"I was just thinking their landscaping looked nice."

"It is, and they hire the neighborhood boy to mow the lawn, though soon I'm sure they'll get one of the grandkids to do it."

"That's great," I said sincerely.

"Only, with her garden? Mom likes to tinker. She tinkers, and then she kills things. Often. So then they try to bring it back to life, but they add more plants while they wait. It's a jungle and a mess and way too much work for them, but they're trying. Don't give them help, or hints, or let them try to see what they should be doing to make their garden look like a professional cares about it."

I shook my head, frowning. "Am I that person?" I asked, and she looked up at me.

"What person?"

"The person that judges random strangers. The person who's going to judge the strangers that will let me stay in their home without warning. Am I that person?"

She cringed. "No. But I'm stressed out, and my mother is kind of notorious for the jungle that is her garden."

"That's fine. If she does ask for help, though, am I allowed to give it? Or should I just say she's doing great?" I was a little worried and intrigued about what it could look like. I wanted to know. It wasn't like I completely revamped every lawn I ever walked onto. That would take too much of my time, and I didn't have time for that. As it was, I had multiple projects waiting for me when I got back, something that I was ignoring for now because we needed to be on the top of our games for this family reunion of hers. I didn't think either one of us was truly there yet.

"You're not that person. I'm sorry. I'm just freaking out over little things because I'm bringing a man to a family reunion. That's not my date. And we haven't... and I'm not even going to finish that statement."

"It's fine. We're going to work it out."

"Yes, we are," she said quickly, as she nodded and looked towards the house. "I'm pretty sure we're going to park in the back later, but they want us to come through the front door at first. So let's make that happen."

"Should I bring the bags now?"

She shook her head. "No, that'll just hinder us."

"I've got you."

She looked at me then, and I wasn't sure I should have said that.

"Let's get inside," she said. She gave me a tight nod, and I felt like we were gearing up for battle. Perhaps we were.

"Do you remember everyone's names?" she asked

as we got out of the SUV. She ran her hands over her body, and my mind went to where it shouldn't. She gave me a look, and I knew *she knew* exactly where my thoughts had gone, but I did my best to ignore it. I was doing my best to ignore more than a few things today.

"I hope you at least wrote it down, because they're going to know everything about you." She frowned. "Or at least about Beckett." She cringed, and I shook my head.

"You did tell them it was *me* coming, right?"

"Of course I did, but they get confused. Your family has a lot of twins."

"We have two. Two sets of twins."

"That's a lot to a family that has none, which is a family of seven kids, without any twins. My poor mother."

"And I thought our family was big."

"You just have a lot more cousins than we do," she muttered as we walked towards the front door. My hand brushed hers, and she pulled hers away quickly as if I had burned her. I ignored the feeling because we didn't have time for it.

The door opened, and a woman that looked like Brenna in twenty years walked out, a big man behind her.

"Brenna, my darling. You're finally here. We've missed you."

Brenna's mom came over quickly and kissed her daughter on the cheeks, taking her purse from her and handing it over to Brenna's father. Brenna's dad just rolled his eyes, kissed his daughter on the cheek hard before hugging her and glaring at me.

"So this is the new one," he muttered.

Brenna groaned. "Dad."

"What? You never bring boys home. You don't give me chances to act like the big overbearing dad."

"I'm sure you've had that all practiced out."

"I thought you'd have gotten all of that out when you were dealing with her sisters." Brenna's mother turned to me. "Hello, I'm Teresa, this is Sam. We're Brenna's parents. And don't listen to anything he has to tell you. He should have gotten his over-protective dad routine out of the way when Brenna's three sisters were married. And honestly, when her brothers were married as well. Lots of marriages and babies in this family." She grinned as she said it, though she did give Brenna a pointed look.

"Thanks, Mom," she said. "Okay, let's get inside before you guys start laying it on thick."

"We would never. We're just so excited that you're here. And bringing a boy."

"It's nice to meet you both. I'm Benjamin," I said, grateful I could even get a word in.

"Oh, we know all about you. Your Brenna's best friend."

"That's Beckett, dear," Sam said. "This is Benjamin. The other one. The twin. Didn't realize they were so interchangeable."

Brenna cringed. "Benjamin is also my friend. And he came out here to hang out with me."

"Whatever you say, dear," her mom said with a knowing glance.

Brenna narrowed her gaze at the three purses on the entryway table that belonged to her sisters, but quickly schooled her features when her mom looked around.

"I didn't realize my sisters were here."

"They wanted to be here with you. Your brothers are here too, but none of the spouses are." Teresa looked over at me again. "We're a lot all at once, and we didn't want to overwhelm you if we started adding spouses and the babies. All of my children are having babies and just growing up, and it's so wonderful, but the house gets quite full."

She walked away, heading toward the noise from the living room, and Sam followed her.

I looked over at Brenna, who just shook her head. "Well, this is going to be fun."

"Is it always like this?"

"Remember how I used to say that the way that your father treated you about work reminded me a lot of my family? Well, it has nothing to do with work, but all about my childbearing years."

"But you're planning on having a baby," I whispered, doing my best to talk as quietly as I could so the others couldn't hear.

She cringed. "I don't know if my family is going to get on board with the whole doing that on my own thing, but we're not going to talk about it with them, okay?"

"Of course not. You can trust me."

"I know I can. It's just, things got weird."

We were standing alone in the hallway, and I didn't think Teresa had even realized we hadn't followed them, and it was tough to think when I could feel the heat of Brenna near me, the scent of her.

"Brenna? Benjamin? Where did you go?" Teresa asked.

I shook myself out of whatever I'd wanted to do. *This was Brenna.* Yes, we had had sex, but it had been a one-night stand, drunken sex. Drunk and consensual sex meant we were never going beyond what we were doing just then. It was never going to happen again, and I was never going to think about having sex with her again. Except all I could do was imagine how she had felt under me and the fact that I knew what that felt like. This trip was going to haunt my dreams forever. Fuck, it was going to haunt my waking memories.

How was I supposed to concentrate when she was just right there looking sexy as hell, and all I wanted to do was lean down and capture her lips with my own?

"Brenna," Teresa called out, her voice a little harsher.

"Come on, we're late," she muttered, and I followed her towards the kitchen area. The house was an open concept, not unlike some of the floor plans that we built with Montgomery Builders, with a Garrett family touch to everything.

The kitchen looked well used, the appliances a little older, but the top of the line when they were bought.

It was a kitchen that people used, and since there was an extensive group of people standing in it, and in the nook beside it, I figured this is where people congregated often.

And here they all were, looking at me—most of them with Brenna's eyes.

I didn't realize how disconcerting that could be for

others to see so many family members at once—people with their own memories, inside jokes, and connected lives.

How the hell had Brenna so easily melded with the Montgomerys? Because I knew we were probably a thousand times worse.

"Okay, you're finally here. I'm sure you two just needed some privacy in the hallway," Teresa said with a wink, and I knew Brenna was once again holding back a groan.

"Everybody, this is Benjamin. Benjamin, this is Joseph, Ellis, Carson, Josie, Connie, and Amelia," she said quickly, rattling them off as if she had done it a thousand times. And she probably had.

"You're never going to remember that." If I remembered correctly, that was Josie. I knew she was the eldest daughter, the second oldest kid since the family primarily alternated boys and girls. She had four kids of her own and was pregnant again. Everyone looked pregnant, and now that I thought about it, Brenna had mentioned that the guys' wives were also pregnant.

The amount of hormones was going to be ridiculous, but I wasn't going to think about that.

Brenna also wanted a baby. As did my ex-girlfriend.

The themes of this weekend were babies and pregnancy. And I needed a fucking drink.

"Nice to meet everyone," I said, not sure what else to say at all.

"You're Beckett, right?" one of the girls said, and I heard Brenna curse under his breath.

"They just said his name was Benjamin. Beckett's his twin."

"I didn't realize you could date twins," the youngest one said, and if I remembered right, that was Amelia.

"Oh, stop," Teresa said with a roll of her eyes. "No more teasing our baby Brenna."

"I thought I was the baby," Amelia said as she put her hand over the generous swell of her stomach.

"You're all my babies."

Teresa leaned down and kissed Amelia's cheek before she gestured towards the kitchen. "We are going to fix up some dinner. We have pasta with squash, and I bought a few store-bought loaves," she said as Brenna winced.

"I didn't know you were doing bread tonight, or I would have tried to bring something."

"And bring us stale bread since you decided to drive here instead of fly?" one of the brothers said, though I didn't know which.

"You bake bread?" I asked, surprising myself.

"You don't know? She's our favorite baker. How long have you guys been together if you don't even know what she does for a living?" one of the brothers said.

"We're not dating. We're just friends. And I'm the cake decorator. He's had my baked goods." One of them snickered, and I did my best not to join them. Well, that would be an understatement, wouldn't it?

"What I mean is, I bake all the time. I don't tend to bake bread at home since it's not my favorite thing."

"You always make bread for us," Amelia said.

"Because I enjoy it, but I enjoy other things better. It doesn't matter. I'll bake for tomorrow. That is when the family reunion is, right? We haven't changed it?"

"We haven't. I know you want to get some done with that, and there was a brioche that you wanted to make, and I wondered if you could make the monkey bread. I know you wanted to make cinnamon rolls for tomorrow, and you have to start that tonight, but I've been craving monkey bread," the eldest sister said quickly, and Brenna rolled back her shoulders.

"I can do that. I thought I was also baking a cake."

I shook my head, my eyes widening as they continued to all talk about the menu.

"You're doing all of that? Tonight?"

"I have a few hours tonight and in the morning. I enjoy it."

"I'll help," I said.

"Really? You?"

"I can knead. I've got strong hands," I said, and could've groaned aloud as the others snickered.

"We're eating dinner first, and we can ignore the fact that my daughter's not boyfriend just said he's good with his hands," Sam said, and I needed to find somewhere to hide.

"First, let's take care of their car, and get their rooms. Separate rooms," the oldest brother said as he glared at us.

I held up my hands. "No problem."

I ignored the wince on Brenna's face as she quickly hid it. We were not doing very well, and I wasn't sure what our next step needed to be.

Somehow, Brenna's family overtook everything. I had no choice in what I was doing. I was just there. We ate, talked about all of their family, and it wasn't awkward that none of their spouses were there.

"The spouses are having a new Garrett dinner," Amelia said as she smiled. "Everyone that married into the family decided to do a huge dinner tonight just for themselves, since they're going to be forced to be surrounded by every single Garrett known to existence tomorrow."

"Sorry we didn't get you in on that," the oldest brother said. "You're going to be surrounded by

Garretts for at least the weekend. And that's a long time when there's so many of us."

"It's fine. If she can deal with the Montgomerys, I'm pretty sure I can handle the Garretts."

"That's just what you think," Brenna sing-songed, and I laughed.

"Hey, you do pretty well with us."

"You're right, but I'm pretty sure we may just outnumber you."

"Now that's a scary thought," I said with a laugh. I ignored the way that her family looked at us and glanced at each other.

Brenna and I were good at being friends and decent about having conversations. Just because we had sex once didn't mean we would do it again, and I wouldn't be a 'new Garrett,' as they called the spouses.

We finished up dinner of the fantastic pasta and I got a quick tour of the house.

Brenna's mother gestured towards the back patio and garden area that was indeed a jungle. She looked proud of it, so that was all that mattered.

"I need to start baking," Brenna said as she rolled her shoulders back.

"I'm here to help."

"You don't have to," she said as she wrapped an

apron around her waist. Why did that apron look hot? What was wrong with me?

"I want to help."

"Okay, fine. I'm not doing all the little desserts, as one of my aunts is dealing with that because she likes playing with chocolate, and I'm fine with that. I wouldn't have time for it. However, usually, I would have baked a cake yesterday, because at this point it's going to take me a few hours in the morning to get it done, but we will."

"Brenna, a few hours?"

"I know, but it's what I do. They want this cake, and it's not an incredibly hard cake or even a checkerboard or tiered cake. As long as I get these in the oven and they cool quickly, we've got it."

"What do you want me to do?"

"Do you know how to knead?"

"Yes, my mom likes to bake bread. You know that."

"Okay, I'm going to be doing this while you are going to bake bread."

"What if I fuck up?" I said as I went to wash my hands.

"You're not going to fuck up because I'm going to be looking over your shoulder and annoying you the entire time."

"Do I annoy you when I'm helping you with the

weeds in your garden?" I mumbled, and she rolled her eyes.

"Of course you do. It's what we do. But it's fine. We can handle this. It's just going to take a few hours."

I looked at her then, at the way that we brushed up against one another as we stood at the kitchen island, and I swallowed hard.

"A few hours."

"We can do this. We can handle it."

And I did not think right then as I nodded at her that either one of us were talking about bread or cakes.

CHAPTER EIGHT

Benjamin

I was up before dawn, mostly because I hadn't slept the night before. They put me in the guest room on the other side of the hall from Brenna's room. One of the brothers had mentioned it had been their room before they had moved out, and they glared at me as they had said it. I had a feeling it had more to do with being near their baby sister than taking their old room. Brenna was in her old room, which still had the same twin bed she had slept in for years, but had been updated to fit another twin bed, and to make it look like a guest room versus her childhood room. And for that, I was grateful. I wasn't sure I wanted to see the childhood room of Brenna Garrett. I had problems enough with my complicated feelings towards her without seeing more of her past.

I crept down the stairs, unable to hear anyone else. Maybe I would make myself some coffee or see if I could stick the cinnamon rolls or monkey bread in the oven. I wasn't the best baker, but Brenna left good instructions.

I made my way into the kitchen and rolled my eyes. Of course, I wasn't the first person up.

Brenna was there, her hair piled on the top of her head, her glasses perched on the tip of her nose, and an apron around her waist. She had her earphones in and shook her ass as she worked on the dough in front of her. I swallowed hard and did my best to ignore the way her butt moved.

I needed to stop thinking about Brenna this way. It wasn't like I had done it often before. She'd always just been Brenna. I had thought at one point she had feelings for my twin, but that hadn't been the only thing stopping me from thinking about her as anything else other than my friend. Sex and relationships complicated things, I knew that. But we had already had sex, and we were quite literally changing our relationship with every moment we were near one another, despite how hard we did our best to resist that.

"Are you just going to stare at me oddly?" Brenna asked as she pulled out an earphone.

I winced. "Sorry, I didn't want to scare you, and then I didn't know how to get your attention."

"Well, you're lucky I don't scare easily." She shrugged and gestured towards the coffee maker. "I already started the first pot, though I'm pretty sure I'm going to need more than one cup to get through the day."

"Thank God," I mumbled as I went over to the coffee maker. I poured myself a cup and looked down at her half-empty mug. "Refill?" I asked.

She shook her head. "Thank you, but no. It would affect my sugar to cream ratio, so I'm going to wait until I finish this cup."

"You're up early." I took a sip and I nearly groaned. It was made perfect, and I knew Brenna had been the one to make it. And not just because she was the only one around, because it could have been on a timer. No, it's because Brenna knew how to make damn good coffee.

"I would say you're up early as well, but it seems

that neither one of us could sleep, and frankly, I have a lot to do today."

"The family isn't helping?" I asked with a frown.

"There's going to be a lot more than baked goods today at the reunion, and the family each has their roles. Mine happens to be oddly labor-intensive right now—and features actual rolls. If I had gotten here earlier, I'd have more time, but this is fine."

I frowned. "Did our night at the hotel hurt your timeline?"

She blushed, and I could've kicked myself for bringing it up, but it was a legit question. "No, I was going to get here yesterday anyway. Maybe I'd have had a couple more hours, but not really. We didn't stop for anything on our last day, and I had scheduled that in. It's more of the fact that I had work to do, so I wasn't going to take time off early to get here, and I wanted the road trip to think. It's not like I can make anything but the cake itself early, and my mom didn't have space in her fridge for me to do so. Either way, it's going to be a lot of work right now."

"Tell me what to do."

She nodded and gestured towards the two large metal bowls. "Wash your hands and get kneading. It needs one more proof, and then we're going to do some baking."

"After I knead, do I need to shape it?"

She raised her brow, and I grinned.

"What, I watch baking shows. The second proof is after you shape things."

"You're right, and I'll do the shaping just because they want one of them as a plait, but the cob you can do."

"I don't know. Isn't that just a sphere of some sort?"

"No, a sphere would be circular all around, Benjamin," she teased.

"Okay, fine. You're right. I'll get to kneading, is there anything else?"

"Cinnamon rolls are in the oven, and now we're going to work on everything else."

"Good, because I'm starving."

"You're lucky I made an extra batch, because my family can eat their breakfast sweets like the Montgomerys eat cheese."

"I'm not even going to touch that," I said with a laugh.

She just grinned, shook her head, stuck her earphones in the pocket of her apron, and both of us went to work quietly.

We worked for about an hour before Brenna's mother walked in, her hair and makeup already done for the day, but she had on comfortable pajamas still. "I was going to see if I could help, but it seems like you brought your own helper with you. I love it. I'm going to start working the eggs and bacon if that's okay, if you don't mind having an extra person in the kitchen."

"Of course," Brenna said as she moved closer to me. I did my best to ignore the heat of her. "Everything else for breakfast is just about ready."

"Perfect." Teresa leaned down, kissed her daughter on the cheek, and then narrowed her eyes. "You're going to shower, though, because that hair, Brenna, honey. And you don't even have your contacts in."

Brenna just rolled her eyes and gave me a look that I didn't share, mostly because I did not want to get put on Teresa's bad list.

"I'm going to shower as soon as I'm done with this. I have flour in my hair from this morning alone, so I figured showering after might be good."

"You're right, you're right, but we still need to look like a respectable family."

"I know, we can't let the cousins outshine us," Brenna said, teasing.

"You think I'm joking, but it's the truth." Teresa met my gaze. "My sisters-in-law are wonderful people, but they're very competitive when it comes to their children. I need my grandkids and my house to look spic and span. By the end, once we're done with the field games and cakes, we're going to be a little disheveled, and that's fine."

I froze, my hands covered in dough. "Games?"

Brenna met her mother's gaze before both of them laughed. "Oh, didn't I mention that?"

I shuddered. "You certainly did not."

"Oh, just you wait, Montgomery," Brenna said with a laugh. "If you thought Montgomery reunions were wild, just wait until you meet the Garretts."

Frankly, that was what I was afraid of.

I grabbed a cinnamon roll and a slice of bacon before I headed back up to my room to get ready. Brenna had done the same, and her parents and siblings and the rest of her immediate family gathered in the house to eat the other goodies.

I didn't find it weird that I wasn't eating with them, considering I wasn't family, and I did need to get ready. I figured Brenna would show up a bit later after getting ready, but I wasn't sure. I needed space to think, and I couldn't do that with Brenna or her family around.

By the time I came back down, things were in full swing. The family was milling about, and I was introduced to the spouses, the kids, and I knew I would never remember everybody's name. As it was, I could barely remember my cousins' and their children's names. Brenna, however, knew everyone and constantly reminded me as she ran around, helping everybody with everything.

She was a force. Bright and bubbly and sarcastic, just like the rest of her family, and they all seemed to get along. Yes, they sometimes dug in a bit about wanting Brenna to settle down, but her immediate family was friendly. They cared about her.

Her cousins, though? Her cousins made me want to gouge out my own eyes.

"I still can't believe you aren't married and pregnant yet," one of the cousins said, point-blank. While everyone else had been alluding to it, I tightened my jaw and didn't miss the way that Joseph, the eldest Garrett brother, glared at his cousin.

"You know me, work before family. I mean, what is a relationship? It's like I'm going to die a virgin," Brenna joked, rolling her eyes.

Her cousin just glared before she stomped off, her husband and three kids in tow.

"I'm going to punch Carol one day. Just out of the blue, one day, I'm going to hit my cousin, and I've never hit a woman in my life," Joseph grumbled.

Brenna shook her head. "You hit me when we were kids."

"Because you hit me first."

"No, I hit you back first," she said on a laugh, and I just shook my head, wondering how they could joke and laugh so quickly after people were just passive aggressive and downright rude to her.

About an hour into the festivities, when the games started up, Brenna looked at me, and I held up my hands. "I'm not playing the three-legged race. You're one of my best friends, Brenna, but I'm not."

"Need to get you a man who cares," another cousin said as he wrapped his leg with a tie to his wife. His wife just beamed and kissed the top of his head. "You see, it's all about love and compromise. It's a little ridiculous that we're playing this game as adults, but we need to win."

"They're just egging us on," Brenna said.

I growled. "They're about to get what they want and have me kick their ass."

Brenna snorted. "No, don't even think about it. I'm not playing. I have to deal with the cake. They can go see who's the best at a game for children on their own, but I want nothing to do with it."

I followed her, shaking my head. "I love my family. We are nosy and always think we want what's best for one another, but hell, Brenna. I don't know how you're doing it."

"Very carefully. And next time we do a reunion like this, which is every year, by the way, I'll be able to have a baby of my own, hopefully. Maybe they'll stop growling at me."

I frowned. "You're not having a kid because you want to prove to other people that you can, right?" I asked, and could have rightly hit myself.

"You know I'm not even going to take that as a bad thing just now because I can see why you would think that, but no. I want a child for myself."

"I want to be a family," Brenna whispered. "I want that joy. I don't necessarily want all the complications that come with sharing that joy with someone else." She winced when she looked at me. "Is that a bitchy thing for me to say?"

I shook my head. "Not in the slightest. You're allowed to want what you want," I ignored the feeling bubbling up inside of me.

I didn't want Brenna like that. Right? We weren't each other's futures. We were just friends. And yet, why did I have to continually tell myself that?

We were in the kitchen now, ignoring the shouts and screams of happiness and competition outside. The cake would be served soon, and others seemed just to be enjoying themselves. Now all I could do was be near Brenna and wonder what the hell was I doing here.

"Thank you for coming," she whispered, and I looked over at her.

"What do you mean?"

"For coming here. I appreciate it. I know my family can be a lot, but then again, so can yours," she teased.

"That's true."

"I'm glad I don't have to deal with my cousins alone. My siblings are a lot on their own, and I could see from the outside how it could seem that they are too much, but I love them. They're just all in a baby-haze right now."

"I don't appreciate the way that they treat you," I said, out of the blue.

She shrugged. "They don't mean anything by it."

I shook my head, anger coming back harder than before. "What if you didn't want children? What if you tried and it wasn't happening? What if you had other issues that people deal with quietly? How is it any of their business?"

I hadn't even realized I was saying the words until they were already out of my mouth. And while her siblings treated her kindly, they still poked at her when it came to settling down and having a future, at least the future they thought was deemed acceptable. I didn't like it. My family might joke around, but anything that could cause pain? They stayed clear of.

"I think if it hurt me, they wouldn't do it."

"Are you sure about that?"

"Maybe. Maybe not. All I know is that I'm doing what I want to do with my life and my business. The others can't hurt me. They can try, but I'm my own person. I always have been."

We were so close then I could feel the heat of her, and I did my best to ignore it, but it wasn't easy.

I looked at her then and swallowed hard. "I should get back out there, go hang out with your dad or something."

She was so close, her mouth even closer. She was so tiny compared to me, but I could lean down and brush my lips along hers as long as she tilted her head up. But why would I do that? I shouldn't do that.

Before I could say anything, my lips were on hers, and she was groaning into me. She tasted of sugar and sweetness, and all I could do is remember what she had felt like underneath me the first time we kissed.

I needed to stop. We needed to stop.

I wanted to spread her out over this counter and show her exactly what she meant to me, not that I knew what that was at all.

"Oops, sorry," a voice said from the doorway, and I cursed before I looked back over at one of her cousins standing there.

"I didn't realize that you two were an item. So much for being just friends," she said as she waved before she scurried off to tell the entire family what she had just seen.

"Damn it," Brenna muttered.

I took a step back, willed my cock to settle down, and shoved my hand through my hair. "I'm sorry."

"Stop saying sorry every time you kiss me."

"How about I say sorry for the time and the place?" I growled, angry at myself, but was lashing out at her instead.

"We can never do that again."

I met her gaze and let out a breath. "You're right. We can't. I'm going to go upstairs. Tell them I have a headache or something."

"That's going to make sense, considering my entire family probably already knows that you kissed me in the kitchen."

"I don't know what to do, Brenna. We can't keep doing this, but frankly? I'm finding it hard not to."

Her eyes widened, and I wanted to curse at myself again. Instead, I turned on my heel, and I walked away. I wanted to kiss her, and I shouldn't. She had her own shit to deal with, and anything that I wanted from her right now would not fit into those plans. They weren't going to fit into mine either. So I took the shit way out, and I went up to my room, closed the door, and I pretended that everything wasn't fucked up.

I wanted to kiss Brenna. I wanted to do a lot more than kissing. But I was the last thing she needed.

I would have to ignore what I wanted. Sadly, I was learning to get good at that.

CHAPTER NINE

Benjamin

Somehow, it was Monday morning, and I headed back to work. After leaving without more than a few words over a week prior, I needed to face my entire family. I had taken a vacation out of the blue, had gone on a road trip with a friend, and I hadn't told anyone why or what had happened along the way. Not that I was going to explain to them what had happened at all. None of them needed to know what had happened. And, if I were honest with myself, I didn't even know what had happened. The road trip back had gone smoother than the trip there. If you could call unending awkwardness smooth.

Brenna and I barely talked to one another. The driver picked the music or the audiobook, and the passenger spent their time on the phone or working. Each of us had portfolios to work on and paperwork to deal with. Neither one of us had wanted to deal with the reality of our situation. Not that I knew the reality of our situation, but there was no changing that.

Brenna had dropped me off at my house, gave me a look, and nodded tightly. We would see each other soon. We wouldn't talk about what had happened. Ever. We wouldn't tell anyone what happened. We would pretend that we hadn't slept together. That we hadn't fucked drunkenly on a hotel bed. We would pretend that I hadn't kissed her again or seen her with her family and wanted to get to know her more. No, we wouldn't be talking about any of that.

We would soon have to talk about why each of us had left town. Because one day soon, Brenna would choose her donor and get pregnant and become a new mother. The family would know that she wanted to be a mom, and they would find out how that had happened, how it had nothing to do with me since we wouldn't be telling them *everything* that happened on the trip.

I would tell my family my decision. Later today, I would tell Laura my decision. I knew things needed to get going, and I needed to start donating. That wasn't a sentence I would typically think of on an ordinary day.

I wasn't sure how all of this happened at once, but now I was walking into the office of Montgomery Builders and pretending that I wasn't freaking out inside.

I used to be pretty good at this, and yet from the way that Paige narrowed her eyes at me, I had a feeling I was already breaking.

"You're early," my little sister said as she bounced over to me. She wrapped her arms around my waist.

I sighed, hugging her back. "Like ten minutes. There wasn't traffic."

I hadn't slept the night before, so I had probably left a little early, but that wasn't too unusual for me. It wasn't like I needed sleep to do my job. I was only manual labor. Even the sarcastic thought that wasn't at all true made me recoil.

"Well, I'm glad you're here. We missed you this weekend."

"I'm sure you did." She ignored the dryness in my tone.

She took a step back and beamed. "You do look well-rested."

Well, I was good at lying about something then, because there was no way I looked well-rested. But one of us was lying, and perhaps both of us were at this point.

"It was a good trip. Brenna's family was just as crazy as the Montgomerys."

Paige rolled her eyes. "That's what she said. I can't believe you went to her family reunion."

"I hadn't planned on sticking around for the reunion part. I just needed a drive." I shrugged.

I needed to tell my family why I had left. Wasn't that going to be an awkward conversation. Maybe I would do it today and get it over with. I had already made my decision, and I would tell Laura this afternoon. If I got the reason why I had left off my chest, maybe they would think I was acting the way I was because of that, and not because I had slept with Brenna and screwed our entire friendship over in a single evening.

And perhaps it was more than a single evening, but I wasn't going to think about that.

"You're here," Clay said as he walked into the essential area where Paige's desk was located, two cups of coffee in his hands. "I didn't know you'd be here today, so I didn't get you coffee. Sorry."

Paige bounced on her toes. "For me?" she asked as

she held out her hands. "Give me, give me."

Clay rolled his eyes and handed over the cup. "It's because I owe you, not because you're my favorite Montgomery."

"I am your favorite Montgomery. You know this. My precious. Mine, mine, mine." She started singing to the coffee and went back to her desk. "Meeting in twenty," she declared, as she answered the phone and took a sip of coffee at the same time. How she did that all at once, I wasn't sure, but my sister was a genius.

"What did you owe her, and what is in that coffee?"

"She helped babysit the kids last night because my regular babysitter got a head cold, Storm and Everly were out on a date, and I didn't want to bother them unless I needed to, and I was stuck on the job site with Beckett until late."

I frown. "Everything okay there? I mean, with everything you just said."

"Babysitter's fine, Storm and Everly seemed to have a blast at their date, and I don't want to think about the details, and Paige did great with the kids. As for the job site? Burst pipe."

I cursed. "Nobody told me."

"I think we're going over it on the notes today. It happened late Friday night, and I guess everybody wanted to let you have some time to yourself on your vacation. We're not supposed to work on vacations."

I snorted. "When's the last time you took a vacation, Clay?"

"Oh, I'm low down on the rungs of the Montgomery ladder. I'll get a vacation when it's good and ready."

"Already slacking off on the job and wanting a vacation?" Beckett asked as he walked in, his gaze going directly to the cup of coffee in Clay's hand.

Beckett's assistant project manager shook his head and pulled the coffee back. "This is mine. You can get yours. I'm not your *assistant* assistant."

"You have coffee. And I want coffee."

"You're an adult who can pour it yourself," I added.

Clay grinned at me. "See? Now you are my favorite Montgomery."

"Hey," Paige said from her desk. "Not nice."

"You're right. You'll be my favorite next."

"That's all I ask." Paige went back to her notes in front of her, and I shook my head, happy that I had gotten a break from the place, but I still missed it.

"Glad you're back." Beckett's words brought me out of my thoughts, and I shook my head.

"Same here."

"You have a good time with our girl?" my twin asked.

I held back a frown. I knew that Beckett didn't have feelings for Brenna. Brenna told me, and I believed her that she didn't have feelings for him. The possessiveness of his tone because of their friendship rubbed me the wrong way though. I knew that it had nothing to do with me. Beckett wasn't overbearing or an asshole to any of Brenna's former boyfriends. Not that I knew of many of them, but there have been a couple, now that I thought about it. However, I just didn't like the way he said 'our girl.' And that was on me. If Brenna ever heard my thoughts? She would kick my ass, and rightly so.

"You're here," Annabelle said as she came over to me and hugged me tightly. "I'm so glad that you're back. We missed you." She kissed my cheek, and I hugged her close before I looked down.

"You're looking pretty cute." It was true. She glowed, and I knew it was only partly due to the pregnancy. Being with Jacob had made her happier, and I was glad for it.

She beamed. "I feel pretty cute. I haven't thrown up once today."

"Praise God," Archer said as he walked into the area too.

I looked around at my family, and my shoulders relaxed. They would understand what I was about to tell them. At least about Laura. Brenna? No, that was a secret I was going to take to my grave.

"We need to go get into the meeting. Come on." Paige tugged at my hand, and I followed her, feeling more at home than I had for a while. Maybe I needed a break from more than just thinking. Because coming back after time away really did make the heart grow fonder.

We headed into the main conference room, where we met with some clients instead of our individual offices. I knew that my family liked to alternate between all of our offices to give things variety, but I was glad that we would be in this big room. Of course, if I tacked on my announcement at the end of this meeting, Clay would be part of it too, but why the hell not? It would give me practice for when I had to tell my parents. I didn't want to keep that a secret from them, and I just hoped they were the ones that would understand.

"I heard about the pipe," I said as I sat down in front of Beckett, and my twin groaned.

"It was ridiculous. It was on the city too, but we were there to help fix it. It's not going to put us back on time because Clay was thankfully able to get down in the mud and help me, but it was a fucking nightmare."

"I'm sorry I wasn't there."

Beckett shook his head. "If you would have been in town, the other projects that you would have been on were on the other side of the city. Fort Collins might not be that big compared to Denver, but it still wouldn't have made sense for you to drive all the way out to the site that we were at. So you didn't miss anything."

"That's something, I guess." I sighed. "How are the twins?" I asked Annabelle as she set her feet up on a chair next to her.

"Being cute. At least that's what I'm saying. I'm currently feeling good today, so I'm going to say I'm happy."

"They better be happy, the way that I'm taking care of their mom," Archer mumbled as he began to rub Annabelle's ankles.

I raised my brow at my little brother, who just shrugged. "My twin is hurting, so I'm hurting."

"Our twin pain doesn't work that way," Beckett laughed.

"See? Twin pain is the one reason I am glad I wasn't a twin," Paige put in. "Still, I was pretty jealous of the whole twin thing. Now Annabelle's having some of her own."

There was a longing sigh in her voice that all of us ignored. These days, that longing had nothing to do with wanting to be a twin but more about a certain person that hadn't yet popped the question. I met Beckett's gaze, and then Archer's, and the three of us nodded. Annabelle rolled her eyes, but I knew she understood. We would have to see what Colton's intentions were soon if he wasn't careful. Yes, Paige would kill us, and no, it wasn't any of our business, but sue us. She was our baby sister. We would do whatever we had to in order to protect her.

We got settled and went to work, going over the plans for the next two weeks and future client meetings. My job was usually at the end because, nine times out of ten, the original plans would change so dramatically that usually the most challenging work of mine would be right when my family was nearly done with their parts. I didn't mind. I got to get my hands dirty and work with what I loved.

Clay got a phone call right at the end, and I took that as a good sign. I let out a breath and looked at everyone.

"If we have a minute, can I talk about something that's not on the agenda?"

Everyone stilled and looked over at me. "Are you okay?" Paige asked, biting her bottom lip.

I reached out and hugged her close, kissing her on the top of her head. We may be at work, but right then, it was a family meeting.

"I'm okay. I promise. However, I figured I'd tell you why I needed to go on that trip."

"Not just to be with Brenna?" Annabelle asked, her eyes bright. Beckett snorted, and Archer just shook his head. "What?" she asked.

I did my best to ignore all of them because if I wasn't careful, they would be able to read the emotions on my face, and that wasn't the subject I was going to get into right then. Or ever, for that matter.

"Why did you go?" Archer asked after a moment.

I looked between them and nodded, knowing I just needed to get it out there. "I needed time to make a decision and some space. I love you guys, but I needed to make this choice for myself."

"Are you sure you're okay?" Annabelle asked as she rubbed her stomach.

I nodded quickly. "Yes. Which is good because I need to be healthy for this." I winced as they all gave me weird looks.

"Laura and Michelle came to me, and we had a discussion."

"Are you joining their relationship?" Archer asked, clapping his hands. "Because that would be hot. We do have menages in the family."

I snorted, shaking my head. "Laura and Michelle

decided to have a baby. I'm not joining their relationship."

Annabelle put her hands to her mouth, her eyes filling with tears, as Paige came over to me and hugged me tightly. "You're going to be the father, aren't you?" she said, as she bounced on her toes and began to dance around the room.

I rolled my eyes and brought Paige close again. "I'm going to be the donor. Not the father. More of an uncle, with the way that they're saying. I'm going to donate my sperm, and there will be some Montgomery DNA out there that is not going to be a Montgomery. I hope everyone's okay with that because it's going to happen."

"That's amazing," Archer said as he moved around the table to hug me tight. "That is so generous. I always knew you were the best of us, but it's a little ridiculous."

"Thanks," I said dryly.

"This is so exciting. I am glad that you decided without us because we probably would have made pros and cons lists," Paige added, and that made me laugh.

"That's exactly what I was thinking."

"You told Brenna this then? To get on that road trip?" Beckett asked as he studied my face.

I cringe. "Yes, she knows, but not until after we were already on the trip. You got a problem with that?"

"Not at all. However, I have one problem with one thing."

"Beckett Montgomery, you better not have a single problem with this," Paige said, wagging her finger in front of him. "He is bringing joy to the world. It doesn't matter that it won't be a Montgomery, and he's not going to raise this baby as a father. There are many ways to make a family, and you should know that."

I put my hands on Paige's waist and lifted her as she let out a little squeal, and I put her to the side.

"You're done then?" Beckett asked, his eyes twinkling.

"Why are you smiling? You're not saying anything nice," she stated.

"All I'm saying is Laura and Michelle had a twin to look at, and clearly they chose the wrong one. I mean, Laura already had to deal with Benjamin once, and now she's with the love of her life. Why not try me out? I am the better twin."

I rolled my eyes as Archer groaned, and Paige let out a little huff.

"Okay, I'm going to have to text Eliza you just said that," Annabelle said with a laugh.

"First off, Eliza wouldn't mind if I had to, even

though we'd have to talk about it first, and she knows I'm the better twin."

I looked at them both and snorted. "I'm going back to work, and I'm going to tell our parents tomorrow, so don't tell them first."

"Do not worry, I want nothing to do with that conversation," Archer said quickly, and the rest of my siblings nodded.

I cringed. "Oh good. I can't wait. You can tell Eliza, though, and Jacob. Hell, even Colton."

Paige narrowed her eyes. "Thanks," she snapped. "So glad you thought of him last."

"No, I'm pretty sure he thought of Marc last," Archer said dryly.

I winced. "I'm sorry I'm flustered. I keep forgetting how many of you are with people. It turns out everyone is but me."

"Aw, well, at least you're going to go spread your seed out into the world," Archer said with a laugh, and all of us nearly gagged.

"Never say that again," I said with a laugh. "Now I need to get to work, I have two phone calls, and then I'm going to go to an early lunch to go tell Laura and Michelle in person."

"Oh, I'm so excited," Paige said as she started to

clap. "Do you think it'd be weird if I learned to knit a blanket for her?"

"You're not even going to learn to knit a blanket for me?" Annabelle said.

"What? Mom's going to do that for you, but I want to help. Oh, is she going to have a baby shower? What can I do? How can I help?"

Archer came over, put his hands over Paige's mouth, and gave me a look. "I'll handle her. Calm her down. She has babies on the brain."

"Thank you." I shook my head as Paige started trying to squeal through Archer's fingers, and I just sighed.

That had gone better than expected, and I knew my parents would probably be okay with the circumstances, but I was happy with the way my siblings had reacted. It was a different situation, but people had done this before. It wasn't new. I'd be able to help out my friend.

Images of Brenna filled my mind, and I pushed that to the side. I did not need to think about Brenna when I was thinking about having to donate sperm. That was crossing a line, and as it was, I didn't need to think about Brenna again because I wasn't sure what I was going to do when I saw her.

After working for a few hours, I made my way to the

same lunch spot I had met with the girls before. Laura and Michelle were there, iced teas in front of them, their hands clasped.

I gave them one look, and Laura began crying, and Michelle lifted her fists into the air. "I knew it!"

"I didn't even say anything," I laughed.

"You didn't have to," Michelle said. "This is...I love you. Seriously. I have never said that to a man before, but I just want you to know that I love you from the deepest part of my heart. You will be a part of this baby's life, and I cannot believe I just said that we're going to have a baby."

She leaned forward, pressed her lips to mine, bringing a laugh out of me. Then she kissed her wife before Laura kissed me, and everybody started clapping, and I knew they had no idea what was going on, but from an outsider's perspective, it probably looked like we were having a lot more fun than we were.

"I am so excited for you."

"I'm so excited that you're doing this," Laura said. "You're going to help us have a baby."

"I'm going to do my best. And not in a weird sense." I cringed as they laughed.

"Well, we can go over all the details later, but for now, let's have a glass of champagne and just talk to one another because soon one of us isn't going to be able to have alcohol for a while."

"Because I should be pregnant," Laura said as she threw her hands up in the air.

We did indeed have a champagne lunch, then I sat with my friends. I might admit this might not be the most conventional way to bring a life into the world, but I was damn glad that I was saying yes.

I was moving forward with my life, making decisions. My thoughts of Brenna and what part of me wanted didn't need to be part of it. We had walked away from each other without saying a word, and that was for the best. I needed her to be my friend. I needed her to be in my life. That meant we had to put what had happened behind us and not think about it again, even if the thought of that wasn't easy. For now, I was making other people happy. I'd find my place in the world—without Brenna by my side or in my thoughts.

CHAPTER TEN

Brenna

My back hurt, my head ached, and my wrists continued to make that little crackling sound every time I moved the piping bag. I didn't care. Today was a big day.

Today was baby day. It cost me a considerable chunk of change, but it was what I'd wanted. I wanted to be pregnant. I wanted a baby. I wanted it for myself. Not for my siblings or my cousins or my family. Yes, they kept making different jokes or comments about it, kind of, but in the end, nothing they said penetrated. I wanted to be a mother. I knew if this try didn't work, then I wouldn't be doing it again. I honestly couldn't afford it. I would turn to becoming a foster mother and then adopting, which were also expensive but wouldn't tax my body more than I was already doing. I had plans, and I would make those plans work.

At least, that's what I kept telling myself.

I was nervous. Then again, I had been nervous most of the day and hadn't been feeling quite well. I didn't have a fever, but I had been nauseous earlier and had even thrown up a couple of times. I knew it was because I was stressed out and hadn't been able to keep anything down because of what would happen later, so I didn't worry all too much.

After I finished this cake, and then the order of specialty cupcakes, I would head to my doctors, and things would take the next step. Part of me couldn't quite believe that this is what I was doing. That this was the next step of my life. And again, I hadn't imagined I'd still be perpetually single at my age, not that there was anything wrong with my age. I thought maybe I'd be on the same path as my siblings and best friends by now.

Annabelle was married and pregnant with twins. Paige was well on her way to getting engaged. We all knew it; we just figured Colton was taking his time, and knowing Paige, if she genuinely felt as if it were time and didn't want to wait any longer, she would ask him herself. That's who Paige was. Someone who took life by the lens and made her happiness happen. I was taking a cue from her, after all.

Eliza was finding her new life with Beckett. She was taking her steps in this dance, and I loved her for it. I would take my own steps. My own chances. Hopefully, soon I would be able to tell my friends exactly what steps I had taken. Yes, I still hadn't told them about my plans. I had wanted it to be mine. Benjamin knew, but he hadn't told his family and our friends either. Of course, he hadn't told anyone about anything from that trip, for that matter, but I wasn't going to dwell on that. Because if I did, I wouldn't stop thinking about it.

I had slept with Benjamin Montgomery. I couldn't forget that. I thought about it every night as I went to sleep and probably would continue to think about it until the end of my days. Even if I told myself that there was no need to, that things would get back to normal. In the weeks since we had come back to town, we had both dived headlong into work and rarely seen each other, other than two times at Riggs' where we had casually not spoken to one another or acknowledged each other's existence.

I had made a mistake. Benjamin would never be a mistake. Not in that sense. That would be horrible to him to even say that. But I was afraid we had truly ruined our friendship because of one night.

And a second kiss.

I would worry about what I was supposed to do or say to make things better later. I would. I promised myself that much. However, first, I needed to get pregnant.

I spluttered a bit as I thought the words, grateful that I was alone in my bakery for the evening. I had two staff members who came in and helped with the big things, and with the minute chocolates and other items that took time and more than two hands, but I usually worked on many of my decorations on my own. I was a specialty cake decorator, was highly sought after, and had a months-long waiting list.

When a magazine had come, had heard about me through a friend's wedding, they had put me on their cover, at least my cake, and the foodie show had even done a spot on me. I might not be famous, I was not a celebrity chef, but because of that, people heard of my cakes enough that I had a business that worked.

Those two staff members would have to help me greatly when the baby came, but I would deal with that. It wasn't going to be easy, nothing, when it came to parenting, was, but I would find a way. I wanted this. I wanted it at all.

I would find a way, I told myself again.

I sat down the piping bag, looked over my work

before I gripped the edge of the table. I should have eaten something earlier, maybe some saltines or something that I could keep down, but I had been too nervous.

I shook it off, chugged down the rest of my water, and went about cleaning up after myself. I had to finish up these cupcakes, and then I could head over.

I knew I should call one of my friends, and I shouldn't be doing this on my own. I was stubborn, and people knew that. My mother had always said that she should have given me the middle name Stubborn, and she was probably right. I wasn't sure who I was supposed to call, because if I did, I would have to explain what I wanted and what goals I had. The only person who knew and understood right at that moment was Benjamin, and I knew he couldn't be the one that I would call.

If I called him, he would come. He would be by my side, and he would hold my hand, and he would make sure I was safe.

I couldn't.

Instead, Sky, my staff member and assistant would help me get home.

I wanted a baby, and this is what I had to deal with. I needed to tell my friends. I needed to tell someone other than Benjamin. I didn't like the fact that I had yet one more secret. After all of our anger and tension over Beckett's secrets, here I was doing it myself.

How was I supposed to be a good mother when I couldn't even follow my own rules and morals?

I sighed, rolled my shoulders back, ignored the dizziness, and set up the cupcakes.

I put them in the walk-in fridge when I was done. Sky would finish up the rest of the order the next day.

I knew Sky would be able to take more responsibility once this baby came, as we had both been discussing her increasing her work and hours in the first place. She didn't know why but hopefully when I told her, she wouldn't freak out. Hopefully, when I told anyone, they wouldn't freak out. Benjamin hadn't.

I shook my head, washed my hands, and then headed out to my car. Soon things could be completely different in my life. My stomach rolled, and I knew it was nerves. So many nerves. I drove carefully toward the office, telling myself that getting a speeding ticket today of all days wouldn't be responsible. I pulled myself from my worries and turned down the street towards my doctor.

I wanted to be a mother, I told myself again. I might be going about it differently from what others might have expected, but I did the unexpected. I was stubborn, like they told me. I was going to do this even if I didn't feel a hundred percent okay today.

I hoped I wasn't coming down with a cold because that meant no baby for now. I shook it off and told myself everything was fine.

"Hi there, Brenna," the admin said as I walked into the waiting area.

"Hi, Candace. It's good to see you. How's the baby?"

Candace beamed and held out her phone. "Her first tooth is already in. I can't believe it. It feels like I just was pregnant yesterday."

I beamed as I looked down at the little ball of cuteness. I had remembered when Candace had been pregnant, and it did feel like it was yesterday. Now her daughter had her first tooth and was grinning with that little tooth and all of those gums at the camera.

"She's gorgeous." I wiped away a tear.

Candice held out the tissue box. "Hormones will do that to you."

She winked when she said it, and since nobody was in the waiting room, I didn't mind leaning forward. "Hopefully I'll have even more hormones soon."

"Crossing my fingers for you, darling."

She handed me some paperwork, and we worked through it quickly before I made my way to the back.

"You know the drill, come pee in the cup," another

nurse said, and I nodded, before I did as ordered, and washed my hands.

I let out a breath and looked at myself in the mirror. "Okay then. You can do this. Everything's fine."

My phone vibrated, and I looked down.

Sky: *We'll see you in a bit. Just let us know if you need us to bring anything.*

Me: *Thank you so much for picking me up.*

Sky: *No problem, boss. See you soon.*

I let out a shaky breath before I put my phone back again. It buzzed one more time, and I looked at the screen, expecting Sky.

Benjamin: *Good luck today. You had told me the date before, and I know we aren't talking about it. I'm here if you need me.*

I swallowed hard and let out a breath.

Damn him, damn him for being so perfect at the completely wrong time. Not that there was ever going to be a right time when it came to Benjamin Montgomery.

I couldn't answer. I wasn't sure what I was supposed to say. Thank you? I miss you? We should talk? None of that was going to work. Instead, I slid my finger over the screen where his name was and let out a shaky breath before I put my phone back in my purse. I quickly turned it off and told myself that he didn't need a response now. It wasn't as if I knew what I was supposed to say.

I walked into my room, where the nurse had laid out my gown.

"Keep your socks on. I know you get cold feet."

I smiled at her. "That is the truth. Although I always find it odd that we tend to hide our underwear when we're in here."

"I do it too, so I don't blame you. It just doesn't seem right to have my underwear thrown about the room like that." She winked, and I laughed, grateful that she was there to ease some of my nerves.

I was so stressed out, but this is what I wanted. And I didn't even have to tell myself this is what I wanted. I knew it deep down into my soul. This was the path for me.

I was making a stand, making my choices.

I changed into my gown and sat at the edge of the bed, my socked feet dangling as they waited for the doctor. I found as time kept going, I wished I'd left my phone on so I could play a game or pretend not to look at Benjamin's name on my text.

I didn't know it would take this long for them to come in and speak to me, because I knew that they had a few things to go over before the insemination process.

However, minutes kept going by, and worries started to creep in.

Maybe the donor that I had chosen didn't work out? Or maybe today wasn't the right day. Could they tell that from urine?

These are the things I should have known beforehand. Maybe if I had told Paige, she would have helped me create an entire three-ring binder worth of notes with essential parts of the process. No, instead, I had kept this from her, and now I was here all alone, naked under a gown wearing only my socks.

I was making a mistake, not with getting pregnant, or at least hopefully getting pregnant, but not telling the Montgomerys.

There wasn't time now. I knew it, but damn it, why was I so stubborn?

The door opened, and my doctor walked in, a small smile on her face. There was something in her eyes I couldn't quite place.

"Is there something wrong?

"No, Brenna. But let us talk."

My toes curled into my socks, and I froze before I swallowed hard. "Is something wrong? What happened? What did I do?"

"Brenna, I'm going to say this quickly, and then

we're going to talk about a few things. I want you to breathe and know that I'm here."

This couldn't be happening. Something was wrong. "You're just going to tell me something horrible, and I have no one here because I hid this from my friends because I wasn't sure what I was supposed to do." I was rambling, but I couldn't help it. I should have told Benjamin to be here. I should have told *anyone* to be here.

"Brenna, we're not going to do the insemination today."

"Why?" I gasped. My heart raced.

"Because you're already pregnant."

I wasn't quite sure what she said after that, as the ringing in my ears intensified, and then she was reaching out for me and then...nothing.

CHAPTER ELEVEN

Benjamin

I looked down at the notebook in front of me and nearly crossed my eyes. Nothing looked right. I wasn't exactly sure what I was supposed to do to fix that problem. The angles were all off, and I knew it had to be me. My client knew what they wanted. However, they also were open to change depending on what was suitable for the property itself. My family was building this custom home for new clients. My job was the massive grounds, only something was off about it. There were far too many angles and not enough levels. I'd already scrapped one set of designs, and they didn't even touch on what the original plans had been when we had gotten the bid.

The house had changed remarkably during Beckett's time with it, as well as Annabelle's architectural plans, so it only made sense my plans would change as well. I needed to go out and get my hands dirty or just let myself clear my head, but today was not about being onsite. Today was getting paperwork done, meeting with different clients, and just getting through our business's paperwork.

"Knock, knock," Paige said from the doorway, and I looked up as my little sister walked in, a bottled iced tea in her hand.

"I thought you could use something."

"Please tell me that's caffeinated," I grumbled as I held out my hand.

"Of course, and I made it, so you know it's going to be good."

I looked skeptically down at the reusable bottle in my hand then back up at my sister.

She scowled at me. "Ouch. That's not very nice."

"I'm kidding."

I shook my head, opened up the bottle, and took a sip. It wasn't sweet tea, but it was an aromatic honey tea and it hit the spot. I took a big gulp and exaggeratedly smacked my lips together as I let out a breath. "Amazing."

"Jerk."

"Hey, I'm sorry. The tea's great. Almost as good as that peach tea you made me."

Paige beamed. "I'm glad you like it. Now, get out."

I blinked. "Get out? Where?"

"Anywhere. Just get away. I can hear you sigh and scowl from my desk, and today is not working. I'm kicking you out because I love you. Play in some dirt. I'm sure there are a few site visits that you can go check in on your team with."

I shook my head. "No, I'm scheduled today to be in the office."

"And we all know schedules can change."

I took a staggering step back, my hand over my heart. "Are you okay? I've never once heard those words leave your mouth before. Do we need to talk?" I was only partially joking at that point.

My sister was the queen of the planners. She knew everybody's schedule off the top of her head, as well as in her paper planner, and her digital one. She kept us in line and was one of the main reasons our company was a success. And she was telling me to go off script. Worry didn't even begin to cover it.

"Paige."

"I just have a lot of work to do, and Colton's parents are in town."

My eyes widened. "Have you met them before?"

"No, not until last night. And it went well. I'm pretty sure his dad loves me, and I'm pretty sure his mother doesn't know what to do with me." She cringed, and I set down my iced tea so I could wrap my baby sister in my arms. I held her close and kissed the top of her head.

"Why do you think that?" I wondered if I would have to kick Colton's ass for letting my baby sister get hurt.

"She just acted as if I was just a normal girlfriend that would be in and out of his life like others. Not the woman that's been with her son for over a year now. I mean, I realize I don't have a ring on my finger, and that's fine. Colton isn't there yet."

I let out a breath and then asked the question that I had wanted to ask but hadn't yet, because it might hurt my sister. However, the time had come. At least, I hoped so.

"So, he's not ready to get married?" I kept my voice low, trying not to spook her.

She gave me a look that told me she knew what I was doing.

"Colton and I just aren't there yet. I know everyone

thinks that any minute now, he's going to get down on one knee and propose, but it's not our fault that the rest of our family seems to like getting married as soon as they fall in love. We're taking our time. And I do have time. I don't need to race to catch up with the rest of the family."

"As long as you're sure."

"I am sure, however, no matter what, that we are serious. I'm a little worried that his mother didn't seem to understand that."

"Did he stick up for you or anything?"

She nodded. "He told me that his mother doesn't want to get close to anyone that she might actually like, and then have to walk away from. His older brother was in a relationship for six years before he and his girl-friend broke up. I think that's why she acts the way that she does. At least, that's what I'm going to tell myself. Either way, though, that doesn't make me feel great, you know?"

"I don't want him hurting you," I whispered.

"It's not hurting me."

I raised a brow.

"It's not," she said with a laugh. "It's more that I'm not sure what I'm supposed to do to make sure everybody knows that I'm okay."

"I think you just did."

"Maybe. Or maybe people are going to continually worry that little Paige is always the maid of honor and never the bride."

"You're my baby sister. Excuse me. I'm not in a relationship either."

"You're a guy."

"Well, that's just sexist of you."

She snorted, reached up to kiss my chin. "I love you, you doofus."

"I love you too, you dork. As for *that boy*."

"That boy is a man."

I didn't like the way that she said man, so I breezed over it. "As for *that boy*, as long as he's treating you right, I'm fine. And he is treating you right?"

She smiled, her face going all sappy, and I honestly did not want to think about exactly why. "He's treating me perfectly. I promise you."

"Good then. We don't have a problem. As long as you're happy."

She smiled at me, and there was genuine happiness in that look. "I am happy. Colton makes me happy. I like what I'm doing. I like that we're figuring it out and taking our time to avoid making a mistake. Would I like to start thinking about children and having a future? Of course. I'm human. I want babies. Yes, my favorite sister and only sister is having twins, and it's making me all giddy and warm inside, but that just means I'm happy for her. Not too jealous of her."

"Good," I said, hoping she was telling the truth. Because I loved my sister, and I didn't want her to be in pain.

"You know, Eliza and Beckett are looking into adoption, right?" I whispered.

"I do. And if they need family letters of recommendation or wherever that goes, I'm here for them. And you're out there about to father a child, but you're not going to be a dad, but I'm so freaking excited for you. You're going to make that family so happy."

"Well, thanks." I could feel my ears redden, and I ducked my head. "That part is already done."

"She's pregnant?"

"No, my part's done. I won't hear for a couple of weeks about, you know, the other thing."

She clapped her hands. "I'm so excited. I don't want to think about exactly why I'm excited with this part of this whole process."

I snorted and picked up my tea. "You know what? You're right. I am going to dig into some dirt and see how my team's doing. Maybe I'll go down to the site and look at it in person. I can't figure out what I want to do to fix it."

"You will. It's what you're good at. You look at

---

what's in front of you, and you find a plan. That's why I love you." She kissed my cheek again and then tapped the earpiece in her ear before she answered the phone. "Mongomery Builders, Paige Montgomery speaking. How can I help you?"

I picked up my things and waved past Paige as her fingers moved like lightning over the keyboard, and I picked up my phone to call my team to let them know I was on my way, not to check on them, but because I needed a break.

By the end of the day, my back ached, I had dirt under my fingernails, but I had a plan. Paige was right. I had needed to get out of my head and just get to work. The sky had been blue, the clouds fluffy and not full of rain to drench us, though I was glad that there was going to be a short storm later tonight to water what we had planted. I hadn't been needed other than as a strong back and willing arms. I had gotten things done. We were ahead of schedule on one site. On schedule on another. I had an idea for the project that had been plaguing me for the past week.

And I knew it wasn't exactly all because of work that I had been doing my best not to focus on outside elements. I was worried about Laura and Michelle. I wanted them to have that baby. And it was going to be weird. There was no lie about that. It was going to be unconventional for me. But perfectly conventional for them. At least that's how I thought about it. Family was what you made it, and they were making a family. My part of the process was technically done. It was just something I was going to have to reconcile with and work towards this new normal. Of course, that also made me think of Brenna, and Brenna and I weren't speaking.

Oh yes, we had met at Riggs' with everybody else, but we hadn't danced, we hadn't locked eyes or done anything normal. If it wasn't for the fact that the rest of my family was dealing with their shit, I'm pretty sure that they would have figured it out on their own. I was surprised nobody had come to me and asked me what the weird undercurrent between Brenna and I was, because I sure as hell felt it.

Nobody had asked. Nobody wanted to know what happened on our road trip because it was as if they never would've thought Brenna and I would've slept together.

Yet, the thing was, I wasn't even sure how it had happened. Hell, between my dreams and the way that my cock kept pressing against my zipper? I wanted to do it again, and that was going to be a problem.

I pulled into my garage and got out, knowing I needed to shower, and I just wanted a beer. I thought about calling up Beckett and heading down to Riggs', but I knew tonight was date night with Eliza. Clay was dealing with a parent-teacher conference for the evening, so he was out. And Lee was out of town at a work function, so I was running out of people to hang out with. Archer rarely came out these days anymore, because he liked staying at home with his boyfriend, and while I didn't mind that, I did miss seeing my brother. Even if Colton's parents weren't in town, I didn't know Colton well enough as a friend to just hang out with him without Paige and the rest of the family.

I was running out of friends, everyone else was moving on with their lives, and somehow I was left behind, and I wasn't sure how I felt about that.

I quickly showered, then pulled on a pair of sweatpants before I walked shirtless out to the kitchen to grab a beer. I had just taken the first sip when someone banged on the door. I frowned before I made my way towards the front. I looked through the peephole. My eyes widened before I took a step back. I opened the door, and Brenna barreled through.

"We need to talk. We need to fucking talk." She whirled and looked at me, her eyes wide. "You need to have a shirt on when we have this talk."

"Hey, Brenna. You're welcome to come inside."

You're welcome to do a lot of things.

I didn't say that out loud.

"Please put on a shirt. We need to talk."

I opened my mouth to make a joke or to say anything to figure out why the fuck she was here, and then I got to look at her. She was pale beneath any concealer she wore. Her hair was piled up on the top of her head, and it looked like she hadn't slept the night before. Honestly, it looked like she hadn't slept in a while, her hands were shaking, and I wasn't sure what I was supposed to do. So I set down my beer and moved forward.

"What's wrong? Talk to me?"

"I need you to put on a shirt."

I cursed her. "I'm not going to put on a shirt and take time away from whatever you need to tell me. What's wrong? Is someone hurt? Is it Beckett?"

Fear slid up my spine, and I looked around for my phone. I had put it down when I'd come in, but I hadn't checked my messages in a while. Fuck. Was someone hurt?

"No, it's not them. No, everything's fine. I mean, it's not fine. I should just come out and say it."

I nodded quickly, my heart racing. "Are you sick? Oh

shit, you had an appointment yesterday? Did everything not go okay?"

I swallowed hard and moved forward, putting my hands on her shoulders. She froze for the barest instant, and then I realized this was the first time I had touched her since our trip. Fuck. What the hell was wrong with me?

"My appointment. Right. It didn't go as planned."

"What's wrong? Whatever happens, I'm here for you. I promise, Brenna. Just talk to me."

She bit her lip before tears began to fill her eyes.

"Don't cry," I said, feeling as if someone had punched me right in the chest. I reached up with my thumb and wiped away her tears. "Don't cry, Brenna."

"I can't...I can't think. Benjamin. I'm pregnant."

I blinked and tilted my head. "You can know that soon after the process? I didn't know science was like that."

In the distance, I swore I heard a bell ringing, something warning me that it wasn't quite where my mind was going. Maybe I was just losing my mind. That had to be it.

"Benjamin. I'm pregnant. I didn't get inseminated yesterday because I was already pregnant. At least a few weeks now. As in, I know the exact date of conception."

I looked at her then, blinked, and took a staggering step back. "Pregnant?"

"I know," she said, her voice going high-pitched. "I know. We used a condom."

"I know. I remember using the condom. I remember taking care of the condom. I didn't see a hole in it. I would've noticed if there was a hole in the fucking condom, wouldn't I?" My voice kept getting louder, and I gulped deep breaths to try to stay sane.

It wasn't working.

"I don't know. We were drunk. And we cleaned up afterward. Oh my God, I was on fertility meds, Benjamin. All so I could get pregnant easier. Your fucking Montgomery sperm came at me."

"What the fuck?"

I began to pace before I looked at my beer and chugged it.

"Oh, good for you. You can have a beer. I can't do anything to calm my nerves because apparently, I'm pregnant. With child. With a Montgomery kid. With your kid. Oh my God, Benjamin. I haven't been able to tell anyone, and it's been twenty-four hours. I've just sat in my house just thinking and looking at my phone and saying I should call you and I should talk to you and then I could do nothing. I ignored all of the girls' calls, and all I did was say I wasn't feeling well. I've been lying to them this whole time."

I sucked in a breath and then took her shoulders again. "Breathe. You're rambling."

"Ramble with me, will you? Panic with me. Oh my God, Benjamin. This wasn't in the cards. This is not what I planned."

"I know. I know. Fuck."

"Exactly. I haven't even told the rest of them that I wanted a baby. That I was on fertility meds, that I was going to get inseminated. By a stranger's sperm. Not my friend's."

My last brain cell seemed to be on life support as I tried to keep up with what was happening.

"We slept together, and now we're having a baby."

Tears spilled down her cheeks again, even as my heart did that little somersault. Warmth filled me, and I let out a breath.

"A baby," I whispered.

Her lower lip wobbled, and she nodded. "I didn't plan on this, Benjamin. I was going to do this on my own. It wasn't going to know the father, and I wasn't going to deal with the complications. And now, what the hell are we going to do?"

I swallowed hard, wiping away her tears again. Brenna was one of my friends. She and Beckett had been closer for many years, but Brenna had been a vital part of my life over time. And we had slept together. We had made that conscious choice, even after a couple of drinks, we had still gone all in, and known we would have to face the consequences of our emotions, just not the consequences of everything else that came with it.

"I don't know," I whispered, and her face fell. "I've always wanted kids, Brenna."

She cringed, nodded. "Me too. That's why I was doing this. It seems you beat those other sperm to the punch."

That brought me up short, and my eyes widened. "Oh God, Laura."

"Is she pregnant too?" she blurted, and she put her hand on her mouth, her eyes comically wide.

"I don't know. They're going to tell me as soon as they find out. Holy shit."

"Holy shit is right. Benjamin. We're not dating. We were never dating. We slept together once, and we were going to never talk about it again and pretend it didn't happen, and now look at us."

"I know. But Brenna? Whatever happens, whatever the two of us figure out with this child, because you're going to have a child, *we* will have a child, we are friends. Friends can be parents, right?"

I literally had no idea what I was saying. It felt as if

one side of my face had gone numb, and there was that ringing sound in my ears, and I was just trying to keep up. Brenna was freaking the fuck out, and one of us had to be calm. And apparently, I was the calm Montgomery. I could not panic, I could not forget, so I had to be solid and logical.

My friend was having my baby.

We had slept together, just once, and now she was pregnant. With my kid.

And I had to be calm.

Somehow I had to be fucking calm.

"Friends can be parents," she repeated. "What are we going to tell your family?" she asked, her eyes widening again.

I swallowed hard. "The truth. Because I have a feeling that no matter what happens, we're going to need them, and I don't think we can lie. I don't think I'm going to ever be a good enough liar to keep this quiet."

She nodded before she took a step back and rested her hands at her side. "I wanted to do this on my own."

I opened my mouth to say something, but she shook her head. "But that isn't what's happening. So now we need to make a plan. Somehow. I'm not just going to hide this baby from you. I'm not a horrible, evil person, and you would always have been in my child's life as one of the uncles or the friends, and now you're going to be the father, and I need to figure out what that means. I'm never going to hide this baby from you. I'm never going to ask you for anything. I just want you to know that we exist."

I cursed under my breath, moved forward, cupping her face with my hands. She stilled and looked up at me. "I was always going to be in your baby's life. Right now? I'm not walking away. We'll figure this out. Friends first always. Friends, as we said, can be parents. I'm not walking away, Brenna. We'll tell the family. We'll tell the others. No matter what happens, it's you and me. We'll figure this out. We have to."

I looked at her, not knowing what else to say, and when she blinked up at me, I wanted to lower my head, wanted to kiss her and promise her and lie to her and say that we would figure everything out, and there'd be no bumps in the road. Instead, she looked at me, bent over, and threw up on my bare feet.

I sighed, pulled her hair back, and she kept throwing up, and I knew that if there was ever a symbol for what my relationship was with Brenna, I was standing in it. Fuck, I was going to be a father.

Now I was a little queasy right along with her.

CHAPTER TWELVE

Benjamin

My palms were sweaty. I wasn't sure my palms had been this sweaty since I was a teenager picking up my date for the prom. Hell, I wasn't sure that was even the case then. Today was an all-new tension and nervousness riding me. We were going to a Montgomery dinner at Annabelle and Jacob's home, where Brenna and I were going to tell them that we were having a baby. This was not normal and totally not in my wheelhouse. Yet, it had to be in that wheelhouse because we had had sex.

I was going to be a father.

I rested my hand on the doorway, knowing I needed to leave, but wanting to take a breath first.

I understood the mechanics of how this had happened, and yet it still hadn't sunk in. Brenna was pregnant. We had created life, and now our lives would be forever entwined, and not merely because we were friends and had the same social circles.

Would it be a boy or a girl? Would they grow up and look like Brenna? With that same humor and wicked attitude? Would they be a little quieter and reserved? Would it be a little girl with pigtails? Or maybe a boy who wanted to learn to garden like me?

I let out a breath, knowing I was getting ahead of myself. I needed to read up on pregnancy and children and what it meant to be a parent. I didn't even know the size of the baby at this point. Was it even the size of a grain of rice yet? Was it smaller than that? When would it be the size of a cantaloupe?

These were questions that I did not have any answers for, and it worried me. I usually had better answers for things like this, yet there was nothing. I was going to be a father. I didn't know if I was ready.

I let out a breath and headed towards my car, knowing I needed to go pick up Brenna so we could show up as a united force. That had been my idea. Not because I felt like she needed me, but maybe because I needed her. Or perhaps because I wanted us to show up as one so we could leave together or lean on each other if things got bad. Not that I thought my family was going to shun us or be cruel, but they could be overwhelming. We were Montgomerys. It was what we did.

I headed towards Brenna's place and tried to formulate my thoughts of how we would do this. We couldn't just blurt it out, but maybe we could lead up to it? We didn't have a plan. Mostly because we didn't know what the family was going to do once they found out. We were going to be in each other's corners even if we didn't know what we were going to do together.

When I pulled into Brenna's driveway, she was already standing on the porch, her cross-body bag over her shoulder, and she kept tapping her foot to whatever music was in her head. She had a dessert box in her hands, so I got out of my truck before she had a chance to move towards me and pulled the box towards me. "I've got this."

"I'm fine. I may be pregnant, but I'm not without strength." She winced as she said it, and my heart did that little leap thing.

"I can't believe I just said that like it wasn't a big deal. Like I'm used to it or something. Holy hell, I'm pregnant."

My lips quirked into a smile even though I hadn't planned on it. "Yes. We are pregnant."

"I'm going to be the one that gets swollen ankles and deals with morning sickness."

I raised a brow. "I'm pretty sure I'm the one that dealt with part of your morning sickness two days ago."

She cringed as we got into the car, and I handed the cake box back over.

"I am sorry about that. It was a lot of vomit."

"Thankfully, I wasn't wearing shoes, so you didn't ruin them." I held back a shudder at that.

"It was on your bare feet, and that was probably kind of gross."

"It wasn't my favorite thing in the world, but it's not the end of the world. I'm here for you. I sort of held your hair back even though I couldn't move you to a place that would be more conducive to emptying out your stomach."

"You did hold my hair back. See, we've got this? We're totally a team."

"We are a team. I'm not going to let you do this alone."

"Thanks," she whispered, before she rolled her shoulders back.

We pulled into Annabelle and Jake's neighborhood. Most of my family lived decently close to each other around here, so it wasn't as if we had that long of a drive, but with the way that Brenna's skin tinted slightly green just then and my stomach rolled, I wished that we would have had a little bit more time on the road.

"So, we don't have a plan," she said as I pulled into the driveway.

I turned off the car and nodded. "Other than just being there. No, we don't."

"I've made cake," Brenna blurted.

I looked over her. "I hoped it was cake. Or cupcakes. Or pretty much anything. I love your baking."

She smiled at me then, and there wasn't a hint of fear or nausea on her face. "Thanks for that."

"It's the truth. You've always known that."

"Still, though, thank you. And like I said, I baked a cake. Maybe we can tell them after we've fed them sugar?"

"We go through the whole dinner pretending that we haven't slept together and we aren't having a baby?" She cringed, but I continued. "If we blurt it out at the beginning, it'll not necessarily ruin dinner, but make it difficult."

"That was my thinking."

"Dessert. Here's a cake, and by the way, we created a new life."

She smiled then. "That makes sense. We've got a plan. A horrible plan that's going to end up with more questions than answers, but we have one."

"They're going to ask us what our plans are," I added.

"They don't need to know them yet."

"As we don't have any plans other than making sure we don't fuck up our friendship or this baby, yes, that's all the plan that they're going to need to know."

"They're going to have lots of questions, and perhaps answers."

"And we'll listen. No matter what, it's you and me. Okay? No matter what happens, we've got this." I reached for her hand and squeezed it, and she swallowed hard, smiling softly.

"We've got this. I still can't believe this is happening, but okay."

I shook my head before I pulled away so I could get out of the truck. I was over on her side, helping her out before she had a chance to fully wiggle down, then she narrowed her gaze at me.

"Your truck is too high."

"I don't even have a lift kit on it. I just leveled it out."

"Still, you need running boards. Can you even fit a

car seat back there?" she asked, and looked at the back of the cab.

I had my hands on her hips as I helped her down off the truck, and I swallowed hard. Mostly because of the feeling of her body pressed against mine, but then again, maybe the nervousness had to do with the idea that we were talking about car seats in my truck.

"We can. It's a full extended cab, but I don't know. Do you want to get a minivan?"

Brenna snorted. "I have an SUV, as you well know since you spent a few days in it. I don't need a minivan."

"I need the truck for work. I could afford to get another car, especially if the truck is for working on the company dime, but hell, I don't know. I didn't think about it. I don't even know what we're going to do about living situations."

She froze and looked up at me. "Okay, first the Montgomerys, and then the rest of our lives. I don't have time to think about the actual logistics of having a child with you."

"Oh good, at least we're on the same level here."

"Of confusion and fear? Good. We're at least here."

"You're here," Annabelle said as she leaned against the doorway, her hands over the swell of her stomach. "And you brought dessert." She held out her hands, wiggling her fingers. "Give me."

"The cake is for after dinner," Brenna said, and I figured if we had cake now, that meant we'd have to tell them about the baby now. And maybe that would be a good thing. Ripping it off like a band-aid.

That was a great way to think of my future child. Something painful.

"That's not very nice. I want to see what kind of cake you made."

"You're welcome to see, but you're not allowed to touch."

"You're just a tease."

Annabelle leaned over, kissed Brenna on the cheek as Brenna surreptitiously handed over the cake box to me.

"Keep it safe, Benjamin."

"I've got it," I muttered, and Annabelle laughed at me.

"You're my brother. You're supposed to be the one on my side."

"Sorry, the cake baker makes the rules."

"Meanie," she muttered, her eyes dancing.

"You're looking good," she said, looking between us and then at my truck. "I didn't realize you were driving in together."

"It's amazing what happens when you hang out with your friends," Brenna said, her eyes dancing as she moved into the house. Annabelle gave me a look, and I shrugged. Thankfully, Annabelle knew me well enough that shrugging was usually enough. She wouldn't have actual questions yet, which was good because I didn't have answers for her.

It seemed we were the last ones to arrive, as everybody was hanging out in the living room and kitchen areas. We had designed this house as a family, and I had done the landscaping on it. While Annabelle and Jacob did some of the upkeep, I did the significant things during the spring. I loved this place. It fit the two of them. And fit the children they were going to have.

Jesus, I was going to have to have a room for my kid in my house. And that kid would have a different room in Brenna's house, because Brenna and I weren't together. We weren't going to raise this child as a unit underneath one roof. We would be living separately, so there were already going to be complications for this baby before they had even taken their first breath.

We were going about this completely wrong, and I wasn't sure how we were supposed to fix it.

"You're here," Mom said as she went up to her tiptoes to kiss my cheek.

"Your dad and Jacob are out there grilling while Beckett, Colton, Lee, and Archer are on the patio, watching the two of them and pretending they don't want to step in at the grill."

I snorted. "Are you telling me that I need to go out there and help them?"

"You mean help annoy them? Maybe."

I frowned. "Archer's here, but is Marc here?"

"He's on his way. He had an emergency at work, so they needed to take separate vehicles, but Archer said that he would be here because they had something to tell us."

Her eyes filled with something I couldn't quite read, and I swallowed hard.

"What do you mean?"

"I don't know. Maybe they're moving in together? Or, I don't know. I do know that Archer seems happy. Therefore, I am happy."

"Good."

I leaned down and kissed the top of her head and then went deeper into the house. Paige was bouncing in the kitchen, helping Brenna and Eliza with some of the meal prep. The guys were indeed back on the deck, but came in every once in a while to bring in different items. They were all working cohesively as if we had done this a thousand times before. And maybe we had. And the odd part was that soon there would be children in this. Annabelle was having twins soon, and then Brenna and I would be joining them.

We were expanding the Montgomerys, just not in the ways that I thought we would.

Brenna met my gaze, anxiety filling her eyes, but I did my best not to stress out or show anybody that I was just as anxious as she was. We needed to tell them that we were having a baby. And I wasn't sure how we were going to do that.

The doorbell rang again, and I looked over my shoulder as Mom let Marc in. Archer came strolling into the living room and looked over at his boyfriend.

"You're here."

"I told you I would be." He leaned down and kissed Archer square on the mouth. "I'm sorry I'm late. However, I'm here. Promise you."

"Good."

And then Archer reached up his hands to push Marc's hair from his face, and my mother let out a squeal.

"Is that what I think it is?" Mom exclaimed, and I looked over and blinked.

"It is," Archer said, his cheeks red.

"You're engaged?" Mom asked, and everyone started talking at once. People were crying, hugging Archer close, patting Marc on the back.

I just shook my head, a smile playing on my lips, as Brenna came to my side and leaned against me. "Well, maybe today isn't the day," she whispered.

I looked at her then and shook my head. "Maybe we wait?"

It would be customary to wait until she was in her second trimester, in case something happened, but we had wanted to tell the Montgomerys as soon as possible because keeping secrets wasn't going to be good for us. And we had a lot of planning to do, and that wasn't going to be easy with keeping those secrets.

I let out a breath, and moved towards Archer, and hugged him tightly. "I'm happy for you, little bro."

"Are you?"

"Of course I am."

"Good, you just looked a little scared just then."

I shook my head and hugged Archer even tighter. "No, that's not it. I'm just really fucking happy for you."

"And you," I looked over at Marc. "You're about to be a Montgomery."

Marc raised a brow. "I'm not sure what last name we're picking."

"Oh, that doesn't matter," Paige said, and she hugged Marc close. Marc stiffened, but I knew that was just because he wasn't a huge touchy-feely guy. Too bad he was marrying into the Montgomerys.

"What do you mean, that doesn't matter?" he asked.

"You're marrying into the Montgomerys. So even if Archer takes your last name, you're still going to be one of us."

"One of us," everyone, including the non-Montgomerys, repeated, and we all looked at each other before we burst out laughing. Marc's lips twitched into a smile before he pulled Archer to his side.

"Well then, that isn't a creepy welcome at all."

"We try," Beckett said, with Eliza in his arms.

Brenna let out a little moan, and people looked towards her before she held up her finger and ran towards the bathroom. I cursed under my breath and followed her. Fuck it. I wasn't going to hide that she needed help or that I wanted to help her, but this might complicate situations.

"Brenna?" Beckett asked as he followed us.

I held up my hand. "I've got this."

"You've got what?" my twin asked, his eyes wide.

I stepped into the bathroom, knelt beside Brenna's shaking form, and held her hair back as I reached for a washcloth to wet it.

"It's fine. I've got you."

"This sucks, Benjamin."

She leaned into me, and I helped her clean up as she let out a shaky breath.

"What's going on?" Beckett asked, and I looked up to see my entire family standing in the doorway, their eyes wide as they looked between the two of us.

"It's nothing. Brenna's just not feeling well."

"You're lying," Beckett said, his voice a whisper.

"Oh my God," Paige exclaimed, her hands over her mouth.

"So, I was going to feed you cake first," Brenna said with a laugh, and I sat down completely on the floor, Brenna in my lap as I helped wipe her mouth after she had thrown up. I reached over, flushed the toilet, lowered the lid, and looked at my family.

"I guess there's a few things we need to tell you," I said, and my mother let out a little squeal.

"Are you serious?" Archer asked.

I winced, feeling terrible. "Shit. I'm sorry. I didn't mean to steal your thunder."

"No thunder stolen at all," Archer added, and Marc nodded.

Marc opened his mouth then shook his head. "This family sure does like to do things big."

"Go big or go home, apparently," Colton said, meeting the other man's gaze.

"How did this...? What is this...? What the hell is going on?" Annabelle asked, her mouth dropping.

Brenna looked at me then let out a sigh. "There's a lot we need to tell you, but Benjamin and I are having a baby."

Everyone started talking at once, and I held up my hands, quieting them.

"We will answer your questions, but maybe not when we're sitting on the floor, and we need to get cleaned up."

"A baby," my dad whispered. "You're having a baby."

"Looks like," Brenna said with a laugh. "Seriously, we'll explain everything that we know. Just give us a minute."

They all looked at each other before they scrambled away, and I knew that dinner was probably going to be on hold, and the interrogation would soon begin.

"Do you want to make a break for it?" Brenna asked, and I laughed.

"I think they'd find us."

"It's true. You guys sometimes suck like that."

"Once a Montgomery," I muttered, and Brenna winced.

"Things are complicated."

"Just a little bit."

"We can't change anything too much. You know? We can't make things more complicated than they already are." I didn't understand what she meant until I looked down exactly where she was sitting and the fact that she kept rubbing against a certain part of my anatomy.

I winced. "Sorry."

"No. It's fine. I just, this wasn't exactly how I wanted tonight to go."

"It's the way it's gone, so we'll figure it out."

"Maybe. Or maybe it will just make things worse."

"That's the spirit," I said as I kissed the top of her head, and she sighed.

"Let the interrogation begin," she muttered.

"Well, the good news is we can always shift the focus to Archer and Marc."

"We ruined it, didn't we?"

"I don't think so, more that we have no plans, and they probably have more plans, so we can make it a family interrogation. Before we escape."

"Escape. Escape sounds good."

I let out a breath and then helped her stand up, before I looked at her then, and I did my best not to want more.

Because that wasn't in the cards, we were going to be parents, not lovers.

We had enough on our plates without adding that.

At least that's what I told myself.

CHAPTER THIRTEEN

Benjamin

I looked over at Brenna before I picked up my coffee. She stared at me, her eyes a little glazed as she drank her decaf tea and blinked.

It was the day after the Montgomery dinner, and I still felt as if we hadn't truly left. Perhaps we were still there, listening as everyone spoke at once, with so many questions and very few answers.

"We left. We just left."

I shook my head at Brenna's words, took another sip of my coffee. Brenna had come over that morning soon after I had woken up, without either one of us saying that she needed to come over. I had been planning on going over to her house, but I had wanted to give her time to wake up. Obviously, that hadn't been needed for either one of us, considering she hadn't slept, and neither had I.

"You were sick. I took you home. And yes, we ran. Ran like hellfire was behind us, and we did not want to have to deal with the questions."

She looked up at me then and snorted. "Sometimes your humor escapes me." She narrowed her eyes, her lips twitching into a smile.

"Sometimes, my humor doesn't make any sense. I don't think I was being funny. There might've been actual flames shooting at us."

"Maybe only flames shooting at me. I defiled the final Montgomery."

I nearly spit out my coffee. "You think you defiled me?" I thought back to that evening, that sweaty night of kisses and touching and everything, and swallowed hard. "You're right. It was all you. You totally defiled innocent me. I had been a virgin. A sweet innocent virgin that had never laid eyes on breasts before."

She tossed her wadded-up napkin at me, and I caught it, shaking my head. "Jerk. Seriously though, everybody looked so confused. I don't blame them as I'm still confused as to how it happened."

"It did happen. We can't take it back."

"I don't want to. I don't think." She frowned as she said it and then put her hand over her stomach. It was still flat, since she wasn't that far along, and I swallowed hard, my instincts kicking into gear.

"I'm not ready for this at all. You probably read all the books and know what's going to happen. I know nothing."

"You'll catch up. You're smart. I have books. So many books."

I shook my head. "And you'll give me titles? Names? I'm going to need a list. Hell, Paige probably already has a binder for us."

Brenna looked at me before we both burst out laughing. "You know, you're not even kidding. Now she probably has a day planner for how you're going to look these next nine months."

"I'm sure she already picked out the baby's college. Hell. I don't even know when I'm ever going to fall asleep again, and she probably already has this down."

She bit her lip. "It's fine. We'll figure it out. I was going to figure it out on my own, and now we'll do it together. Just not *together*."

I swallowed hard, ignoring the odd feeling of disappointment, because this was for the best. Us not being with one another as we dealt with the ramifications of what had happened.

"I need to head into work; I have a big cake coming in today that I need to work on, and I need to start training my replacements."

"Oh shit, yeah. Because you are your own boss."

"And my maternity leave means that I might lose business if I'm not careful and plan ahead. Maybe I do need Paige to work for me."

"I'm sure she would," I said softly, before I let out a breath. "We'll figure it out."

"I know we will," she said softly. "We're not going to have another choice. Eventually, we're going to have to get answers to your family. And mine." She paused. "Oh my God, I didn't even think about telling my family. I was so worried about the Montgomerys I forgot about my family."

I smiled. "We Montgomerys tend to do that."

"Well, crap. They're going to know. They're going to know precisely when it happened, and they're going to think somehow they're behind it."

"They weren't, though. It's just you and me." I ran my hand down her face, wondering what the hell I was doing.

"That is a lie. It can't be just you and me. We have two extensive and invasive families. They may be excellent and outstanding and will help us with everything, but they're not easy."

"I know. However, we'll deal with it."

"I don't know what 'deal with it' means. So, for now, I'm going to pretend that I know what I'm doing. We all know that's not the case, and then we will figure out what to tell everybody else. They're going to want more answers than 'it just happened.' We don't know what we're doing, but we're going to make a plan."

"Those are pretty much the words we said, and then we ran out of there."

"We're going to need to make it up to Archer and Marc as well."

That made me wince. "You're right. I know we were planning on telling my family last night so there would be no more secrets, yet I kind of wish we wouldn't have. We should have tried to hide it at least another day."

"Maybe I can bake them a cake. They like cake."

I played with the edge of her hair, needing to touch her and knowing I shouldn't. "They do. They love your cake."

"You didn't mean anything dirty by that?"

"No, but now I'm thinking dirty things. I'm sorry. You brought it up."

Her gaze went to my dick, and I groaned, adjusting myself. "That's not what I meant either."

"We used to be able to tell dirty jokes without thinking about one another like this."

"Brenna," I said, exasperated. "I've always had the hots for you. There. I said it. You're hot. But we've been friends, so therefore I've never really let myself think beyond that. But I wouldn't have slept with you if it had never crossed my mind before. Is that what you wanted to hear?"

I knew I was probably saying all of the wrong things, but I couldn't take it back.

"Well, I guess if we're being that honest, I've thought about it too. And not just because you're Beckett's twin. That got weird. I'm not into twins. I swear."

She looked at me then, and I snorted. "You'd be surprised how many people are."

"It's not me. I swear. Now, we're going to figure this out. Just not now. Then I'm going to make Archer and Marc a cake, and we're going to apologize for ruining their night."

"I'd say maybe we'll help host an engagement party for them, but I think we need to start saving money. College is expensive."

Brenna's eyes filled with tears, and I cursed before I

went around the island. I hugged her close and kissed the top of her head. I couldn't help it. This was Brenna. *My Brenna.* "I'm sorry."

"No, it's fine. I don't know if it's hormones or just lack of sleep. But it's starting to settle in. This is real."

"As real as it gets."

My phone buzzed, and Brenna let out a laugh. "It's Laura. You should probably answer that."

I cringed. "Oh, God. I forgot, yesterday was their big day."

"As in?"

"As in, they were going to find out if she's pregnant or not. Holy fuck."

Brenna's eyes widened as I answered the phone and tried not to sound like the world was crashing around my ears.

"Benjamin? We're pregnant! It worked. We're going to be moms. And you're going to be the best uncle. How amazing is that? I'm just so excited for all of us. Michelle's over here crying, or she would take the phone from me, and I just keep babbling. I'm going to have a baby. We're going to have a baby. I love you so much. You have no idea how much this means to us— anything you need, ever. We're here for you. I love you so much. Now I got to go. My wife is crying, and I'm pretty sure she wants to make out. We're having a baby!"

"Congratulations," I said, and then the phone went dead.

She hadn't even let me say anything else; I wasn't even sure she had heard me say anything at all.

I looked down at the phone and then at Brenna, as her eyes widened impossibly. "Your sperm is amazing."

I burst out laughing. "Oh good. That would be something I put on my business card. Master of landscape architect, and—"

"Masturbator?" Brenna cut in, and we both burst out laughing.

"Good, we can laugh through this. As we figure out whatever the fuck we're going to do."

"Okay, we both work, we make plans, we say we're sorry to your family, and then we tell both of our families in truth everything that's going on."

"And friends first," I said, even though some part of me knew that that wasn't exactly what I wanted. I didn't know what I wanted, but I didn't think friends would be the only answer.

I wasn't sure, and I was afraid that I was going to make another mistake. I didn't say anything.

"I don't know if I'm ready for this, Benjamin," she whispered.

I froze, looking down at her. "You're the readiest person I know."

"Maybe. Or maybe I am losing my mind."

"I'm here, Brenna. For everything."

She nodded, and without another word, I helped her to the front door. I wasn't sure what there was to say. I was afraid that if I kept speaking, I would say too much. So instead, I let her walk away and told myself that this was for the best. Even though I wasn't sure that was the case.

I had just gone back into the kitchen to clean up our mugs when someone banged on the door.

I opened it without thinking, figuring it had to be Brenna. "Did you forget something, Bren?" I asked, and dodged my twin's fist.

"What the fuck?" I asked, scrambling back.

"That's my question," Lee said as he pulled Beckett back, and Archer moved in, pushing me away.

"Why are you pushing at me? Beckett just threw a punch at me. What the fuck, man?"

"Just in case," Archer mumbled.

"What the hell? You got Brenna pregnant? What the hell is wrong with you? She's our best friend. You can't just fuck our best friend."

I blinked at him. "It wasn't like that, and watch your tone when you're talking about Brenna."

"Sure as hell sounds like it. A one-night stand on some seemingly mysterious road trip, and suddenly she comes back pregnant? We can do the fucking math, Benjamin. What is wrong with you? You know Brenna. She's sweet and caring and a wonderful fucking person. You don't just do that to her."

"Okay. We were going to come over here to talk to you and figure out exactly what happened without your parents around," Lee said, his voice calm. Probably too calm. "I see we may have come prematurely."

"I have a joke about that, but I don't think this is the right time," Archer put in.

I cursed under my breath. "I'm shocked that Jacob isn't here with you. Or Colton, or Marc. Hell, bring everybody here to kick my ass. Maybe I deserve it."

"You sure as fuck do. It's our Brenna, Benjamin. She was always off-limits."

I narrowed my eyes, annoyance gone, rage taking over. "So you wanted her? You marked her as off-limits to yourself even though you wanted her, and now it's a thing? What's your deal, twin of mine?"

Beckett leaned closer. "I never wanted her like that. That's the whole point. We're friends. You don't fuck friends."

"Well..." Lee said, and Archer snorted.

"Yeah, we don't say that because a lot of our friends

tend to fall for one another. However, we're going to be calm and rational about this." Archer looked at me. "Jacob is at the sonogram appointment with Annabelle. Everything is fine. It's just a routine appointment. Colton is working, as is Marc. I'm sure they would have loved to be here for the show. Dad isn't here because we decided not to be here with the parents where you'd have to explain to our mom and dad why you chose to sleep with a girl who's been in our lives for what seems like forever and get her pregnant."

I somehow followed all of that and growled. "I didn't decide to get Brenna pregnant. It happened."

"Do you not know how to use a condom? I'm pretty sure we went through the same talk with dad."

"What is your problem?" I glared at Beckett. "Why are you acting like this?"

"She's our best friend," Beckett shouted, and pinched the bridge of his nose. "I hurt her before. By not telling her everything, not opening up to her when I got hurt, and then you just come in and, what? Sleep with her?" He let out a breath. "She's our Brenna, Benjamin."

I pressed my lips together. "Brenna and I have nothing to do with you. I'm sorry that might hurt your delicate sensibilities, but you are not part of the equation, Beckett. You have never been, other than being my brother and her friend. I needed to go on that road trip because I needed to think. I needed to think about what I was going to do about Laura and Michelle." I didn't mention that they were also pregnant because that was not going to help the situation. "Brenna had her problems, and one thing led to another, and we slept together. It was mutual consent, something we both wanted at the time. We're friends now. We're going to stay friends. Somehow, we're going to raise a fucking baby. Don't you go to Brenna and make her feel like she did something wrong, because she didn't. We made a choice, and now we're dealing with what's happening. We don't have a plan because this is still new for us. We would like it if you would stop being a fucking asshole and get over yourself."

"I'm not the asshole here," Beckett grumbled, but there was no heat in it. "Brenna?" he asked incredulously.

"Yeah, Brenna. I wasn't expecting it either. But here we are."

"Here we are," Archer said.

I cursed under my breath and turned to my brother. "Congratulations."

Archer beamed. "Thank you. That wasn't exactly how we expected to tell everybody. I had just put on the ring again once I heard the doorbell, knowing it was him. We were going to make it a whole thing. And then it became a whole thing."

"I'm sorry. This might spoil everything, the surprise, but Brenna is baking you guys a cake."

"Well, Brenna's making it up to me, and I'm sure you can help make it up to me by helping us move."

"You're moving?" I asked, frowning.

"I'm moving into Marc's place. That was part of the whole thing we were going to tell you guys about, but yay. I'm getting married. Moving in with my fiancé. Not just my boyfriend, but my fiancé. Now everybody's getting married or having babies or long-term relationships and look at us. The Montgomerys are growing up."

"We're growing up all right. I still can't believe it," Beckett said, looking at me. "I'm an asshole."

I cringed, then realized that I needed to lay it all out there. At least my part. "By the way, before you try to punch me again, Laura called. She and Michelle are having a baby. It's been a big day. A big week if you will."

Lee looked at me then, his eyes wide, before he burst out laughing. "Go you and your sperm."

"Let's not."

"I bet Brenna could bake a cake shaped like a sperm," Archer said. "Not for Marc and me, mind you, but for you. A 'thanks for getting me pregnant, you asshole. Here's a sperm cake' cake."

"No, no," Lee replied, shaking his head. "Little sperm cupcakes all leading to a giant egg cake.

"Oh my God, I am texting Brenna right now," Archer said, whipping out his phone.

"Please don't," I muttered.

"There's no stopping him," Beckett said as he met my gaze. "That's a lot, Benjamin. You're having a kid."

My knees nearly went weak, and I swallowed hard. "I know. I have no idea what the fuck I'm going to do about it, you guys. When I say this is unexpected, it was unexpected for everybody. I'm not just going to walk away. That's going to be my child, just like it's Brenna's. So the whole being a father thing, that's something I'm going to have to deal with and learn, but I will do it. I'm not walking away."

"Never in my mind did I ever think you would," Beckett said softly.

"Thanks," I whispered. "As for Brenna? I don't know what the hell I'm doing there, guys. Everything was just so unexpected."

Lee reached out and squeezed my shoulder. "We all have to get to work, but afterward, let's go to Riggs' and get drunk. And then you can tell us exactly what happened on that road trip."

"I'm not giving you details," I mumbled, my lips twitching.

"Fine, be the spoilsport. It seems like I will be the odd man out, the single one forever."

"Brenna and I aren't together," I frowned.

"For now," Lee said, with a shrug, and I glared at him. "What? I'm just saying. You're having a baby with that woman. You're friends with her. You like her. You never know. One thing could lead to another."

"It would be stupid for us to let one thing lead to another."

Beckett just glared at me, as Archer beamed as his thumbs moved like the wind as he texted.

"It was probably idiotic to sleep with one of your best friends on a road trip. But you did. And I have a feeling that staying away isn't going to be as easy as you think it is."

I looked at Beckett and blinked. "Didn't you just almost hit me and tell me to stay away from her."

Beckett shook his head. "No, I almost hit you because I was pissed off that you got our friend pregnant, and it seemed out of the blue. Now my being an asshole is over, and we're not going to tell Eliza or anyone else what happened."

"Oh, they already know," Archer said, and all of us started to glare at Archer.

My youngest brother looked up and shrugged. "What? I'm in the group chat. I annoyed them until they let me in."

"What are you telling them?" I asked slowly, my words precise.

"Nothing. Just a play-by-play. Brenna's going to kick both of your asses later, but I did not mention anything about what feelings you may have for her because I'm not going to ruin whatever relationship you have."

Beckett groaned as Lee began laughing, and I let out a breath. "Oh good. I'm so glad that everyone can mock the situation that I'm in."

"It's either mock it or cry. I'm pretty sure that Archer might be getting a cake out of the deal," Lee added.

"Great. Cake will fix everything." I ran my hands through my hair. "I don't know what's going to happen with Brenna and me. Our motto is friends first."

"I've seen enough movies and been on enough dates to realize that one of two things is going to happen," Lee said, sounding far too wise. "Either you two are going to make this work for a while before you blow things up and walk away from each other and only see one another for the kid, or you're going to fall madly and passionately in love, and we're going to have yet another Montgomery wedding."

"Seriously?" I asked Lee.

Lee just shrugged. "It's written in the cards, man. You done fucked up. Now you're going to have to deal with it."

I sighed, pinched the bridge of my nose, and knew Lee was right.

CHAPTER FOURTEEN

Brenna

I couldn't figure out why I was nervous. It wasn't as if this were a date. Benjamin was coming over so we could have dinner, try to relax after a very stressful day at work, and make a plan.

A co-parenting not-dating-or-sleeping-together plan.

I probably had to work on the title more.

I looked down at my notebook in front of me, at the very detailed note, and cringed.

"Yes, I have to work on that title a bit more."

However, it was a start because I was not going to make the mistake of falling for the father of my child.

I swallowed hard and put my hand over my stomach. I was far too early in the pregnancy to feel a bump or even a little kick. The baby was so tiny right now. No one would know I was pregnant, except that it was hard for me to keep food down.

Considering I worked at a bakery and was around cake and sugar at all times, it worried me that I kept getting nauseous. However, sugar didn't send me over the edge. Meat, grains, vegetables, fruit, or anything healthy, I had to throw up right away. Cake and frosting? Not so much.

Either this baby would come out with a sweet tooth, or they were nice to their mommy at work.

"Mommy," I whispered, a smile sliding over my face. I was going to be a *mommy*.

While Benjamin was the daddy. To say that this wasn't what I had in mind when I planned this part of my life would be an understatement. It wasn't even close to being any part of it.

Yet, here I was, doing my best to pretend that I was okay.

The doorbell rang, and I pulled myself out of my thoughts and wiped my hands on my jeans. Today was just for planning. The future. Not about what future I thought I would have.

That dream was long gone, and now I needed to focus on what I could change, which meant not concentrating merely on myself. After all, I wasn't going to be focusing on myself alone when it came to having a child.

I let out a breath and made my way to the front door, looked through the peephole, and I didn't relax. Instead, a new tension rode me, and I was afraid, not of Benjamin, but of what he represented.

I'd wanted him. Damn it. Even though I told myself I shouldn't, and it would be a horrible mistake, I did. I had wanted him before, and I wanted him even more now, and with the complications that were our life, wanting him at all would be a terrible mistake. I should know better. Only I couldn't.

I opened the door, and Benjamin stood there, a single lily in his hand and a bottle of sparkling cider. "You know me and flowers. I usually bring plants over to people, but I wasn't sure if you'd like the whole thing or just a single flower, so I went with this. And the sparkling cider sounded pretty good. For me. You can get your own." He winked as he said it, and he sounded as nervous as I did.

I took a step back and blushed as he handed me the flower. "It's beautiful."

"I've given you prettier flowers over the years, but sometimes the single flower does the trick."

"I'm sure you know the Latin names of everything."

"Clematis occidentalis."

I rolled my eyes. "I could tell you how to bake a cake without having to look at a recipe, so that counts for something."

"I like cake. That makes me happy."

"Dinner is in the Crock-Pot. It's some form of chicken stew that I could easily begin this morning before I headed to work." My stomach rumbled, and I groaned. "Hopefully, I'll be able to eat it."

"Let me stick this cider in the fridge, and I'll help you set the table."

"Oh, I didn't even think about that. I was mostly just thinking I'd eat at the sink like I usually do."

He raised a brow. "That's how you eat dinner?"

"I'm a single woman living alone. It's what I do."

"You're not going to be living alone for long."

For some reason, it took me a moment to register that he was speaking of our child and not him moving in with me.

He must've seen the confusion on my face because he winced. "I suppose we should make true plans instead of you thinking I'm just going to move in here. Although I think my house is bigger if that's the path we take, and I have two extra rooms."

"Because even Montgomerys like to build big," I grumbled. "And we're not moving in together, Benjamin. We're not even going to sleep together again."

He raised a brow, and I put my hand over my mouth before setting the flower down.

"I'm going to be sick," I grumbled. My bare feet slapped against my wooden floors as I ran to the bathroom and threw myself in front of the toilet, vomiting the lunch that I had been able to keep down for longer than usual.

I heard Benjamin moving around behind me, and then he was at my side, holding my hair back and pressing a cool washcloth to the back of my neck. I sighed in relief, even before I threw up again, and cursed at myself. "I hate this. Why is morning sickness not in the morning?"

"Have you been able to keep anything down?" he asked, his voice soft.

"Cake."

"Brenna," he muttered. "You know that could be a sign of something wrong."

My gaze shot to his, and fear filled me.

He cursed again. "I know that there's something that women can get where morning sickness affects you more than others. If you aren't able to keep anything down, Brenna, you should tell your doctor."

"You don't have to growl at me and order me around." I knew I was pouting then, but when he wiped my face with a wet cloth, I narrowed my eyes at him. "I'm not an invalid."

"You're not, but you're not feeling well, and it's partially, or perhaps mostly, my fault at this point. Let me help." He paused, his throat working as he swallowed hard. "*Let me help.*"

I wanted to cry or pout or scream. Were the hormones this severe so early in the pregnancy? "I wanted to do everything on my own, but I don't think I'm going to get to now."

"You weren't going to have to do anything on your own before. We would all have been there for you."

"This isn't exactly how I wanted to be having this conversation. This isn't exactly how I wanted any of this to work out. I wanted to be a mom. And here I am, having to deal with the fact that I'm going to have to share." I put my hand over my mouth and nearly gagged on my own self-indulgence. "I'm sorry."

"Don't be sorry. We screwed up the curve," he grumbled. "I'm the one who got you pregnant. While we were both there for the adventure, because damn straight, it was one fucking amazing adventure, you're going down a different path. Yes, you're going to have to share."

"It just sounds so selfish."

"You're allowed to be selfish for a minute. And then you'll do what you do best and make some plans, and we'll figure this out."

"It's not just a road trip. It's a future. It's a life."

He held out his hands, and I slid mine into his as I let him help me up. "See right then? You let me help you up. Let me help you."

"How about I just brush my teeth, and then I figure out what I need to do."

"We figure out what we need to do."

"I stand corrected."

He let me have some privacy, to clean myself up and brush my teeth. I let out a breath, my hands clinging to the edge of the sink. I needed to be better at this. I needed to focus on what I was doing and set boundaries. Boundaries would help with everything. Mainly because every time he was near, I couldn't breathe. When had this happened? When had I started looking at Benjamin that way? I needed to stop. Even before getting pregnant, I needed to stop thinking about him this way. Only I couldn't.

And now I was afraid that everyone had been wrong when they had said I had fallen for Beckett. That they had gotten the wrong twin.

And now I didn't know what I was supposed to do.

I made my way out to the kitchen, where Benjamin stood, spooning bowls full of white chicken stew that I hoped to keep down. He also had a massive plate of crackers next to the bowls, and I grinned. "Crackers, I hope I can do. If not, I'm going to have to feed this baby solely cupcakes."

He shook his head as he set the ladle down. "I don't think cupcakes are going to do it for long."

"Cupcakes are the best. I've been thinking about which ones to make for Archer and Marc."

"We should be seeing them this weekend if you take my parents up on their offer."

I cringed as I sat down next to him. His parents had called me that morning to ask if I wanted to come over for a family dinner, one where we could talk peacefully, and I hopefully wouldn't throw up everywhere.

They were going to have a separate engagement dinner for Marc and Archer, so that way each person had their special celebration.

It still felt odd to me that I felt like I was part of their family after all this time, and yet things were completely different now.

"You think you can eat something?" he asked softly.

"Maybe. Annabelle doesn't get this sick; I'm kind of annoyed at that."

"Well, that just means Jacob doesn't get to hold her hair back like I'm doing for you."

I stirred my soup with my spoon and looked up at him, shaking my head. He took a big bite of soup and groaned. "This is amazing. I mean, I know you're the best baker out there, but I always forget that you're a damn good cook, too."

"There are better cooks out there, Colton for one."

"He's cooked for you?" he asked as he ate another bite.

"He's tried a few different recipes on Paige and us. Mostly for girls' night. I'm surprised he hasn't done one for guys night with you guys."

"Our guys' nights are usually at Riggs', or if it's at one of our houses, he and Marc don't always show up. It's weird, but I feel like we Montgomerys might stress them out."

I snorted. "You stressing out a guy? I am shocked."

"Hey, we're not too bad."

"You are, but it's fine. I'm used to you. Well, at least I was comfortable until I got pregnant by one of you, and now I feel like I'm the one invading the Montgomerys."

"You know it's not like that. Yes, the family has questions, but we are doing things a little unconventionally."

"Is this where we make plans?"

"It can be."

"I know we said we're going to be friends first," I muttered. "And I want to keep that. But what are we going to do?"

"Let's start with the basics, and then we can get to all the complicated things that we'll probably change a thousand times."

"Basics? Like what?"

"Well, we're very good at being professional about this and acting like adults and not freaking the fuck out. So let's start with the easy thing. Work."

"What, you expect me to give up my job?" I growled.

He held up both hands, his eyes wide. "No. We both own our businesses, meaning taking time off isn't easy. But you said you were working with your assistant?"

"Yes, but I'm still making sure everything's going to work out with that. I need someone to take the reins for me when I'm unable to be there. I'm not going to have a full maternity leave, I know that, because I am my boss, but there are some things I can hand off to my crew."

"I can help, too. I mean, I don't know if paternal

leave will work for me because I do own the business, but Timothy and Kennedy both have been taking up more responsibility on the job. So if I do need to take a couple of weeks off, I can, and I want to."

"You'd do that?" I asked, my voice soft.

"Of course. I want to help. And help isn't even the right word. I want to share in the responsibility and share in everything that happens. Like childcare? I have an answer to that."

My eyes widened. "Are you going to bring the baby to work? Just hang out with them out while you're shoveling?"

"I do more than shoveling, but that was what I was thinking. Yes, when they're younger, we can bring them to our offices, but the family and I were thinking, since Annabelle's going to be having twins, I'm having a baby with you, and Eliza and Beckett are thinking about it, and who knows what's going to happen with Paige, and then Archer, our family is growing, so we're going to add a childcare part of Montgomery Builders."

My eyes widened, even as I blinked back tears. "Just like that. As a family, you've decided to what, take a room and make it a nursery?"

"For now, with childcare professionals with us if we can make it work. Eventually, it will be a daycare center for the Montgomerys and anybody that works there.

We've been trying to get it to work for Clay, even though his kids are a bit older. It just hasn't worked out yet because Clay hasn't needed it. If he does need it, we want to be there. Annabelle is already on that, though, so therefore childcare, we've got."

"That would be amazing," I said, stuttering. "Even though I'm going to be kind of sad that I'm not going to be there."

"You don't work too far away from me," he muttered.

"Maybe not, but it's going to feel that way, isn't it?"

"Then we'll make a plan. I'm not saying we have to hide our child in Montgomery Builders, and you'll never come over and visit. But it's an option. When you're ready to get back to work, it's an option."

"It's a wonderful option, and I feel like I'm going to cry."

"Don't. I'm here for you."

"You are, aren't you," I whispered.

"Yes. I am." He moved over and pushed my hair back from my face. "Are you feeling better?"

"Maybe. I don't know if I can think about anything else. Like where to live or schools or names or anything. Just that is a weight off my shoulders, and yet it's terrifying at the same time."

"We keep talking about this as if it might be that

road trip," he said after a moment, and I looked up at him.

"What?" I asked.

"We're so polite with one another, making sure that we don't step on each other's toes as we try to find a path that works for this co-parenting thing. I'm scared, Brenna. We're having a fucking kid, and I know we have so much to do and yet all I can do is think about the fact that I want to kiss you."

I blinked up at him, shocked. "Right now? That's what you're thinking about?"

"Yes. I'm a fucking asshole. Brenna, I've wanted you for a long damn time, and yet I've never really thought about it like that because I wasn't supposed to."

"Because you thought I was in love with Beckett."

"That, and you're my friend. I'm not supposed to want you more than I already do, and yet if I were to kiss you right now? It would be the exact wrong thing to do."

"Completely wrong. As in, we shouldn't. Ever."

I was sitting on a stool in my kitchen, with him standing between my legs, and I knew if I kissed him, it would be wrong.

Very wrong.

So I slid my hands up his chest, cupped his face, and I kissed him.

He groaned into me, wrapping his hands around my hips. "We need to stop. This is just going to complicate things."

"Very much. This is going to be such a stupid fucking mistake," I mumbled against his lips as I kissed him harder. He lifted me into his arms, and I wrapped my legs around his hips, grinding into him. I didn't want to think. Nothing was going the way that I wanted it to or how it should, so why couldn't I just feel for just this moment? We could make this work. We could just have fun, and we could make sure we focused on our responsibilities. We were good at this.

And I knew if I kept lying to myself, maybe it would make sense, but right then, I didn't care. I just kept kissing him. He sat me down on the dining room table, and I moaned into him, needing him. He slid one hand up my chest, cupping my breasts, and I arched into him, groaning as his thumb slid over my nipple.

"You're so fucking hot," he muttered.

"This is very wrong," I muttered as I tugged on his shirt.

"Very much so, but we've already seen each other naked. We've had sex. This isn't complicating the situation because it's something we've done before."

"Oh good, your rationalizing sounds exactly like mine."

And I kissed him again. We pulled his shirt over his head completely, and then I scraped my nails down his body, groaning at the sight of him. He was all chiseled muscle in an eight pack, one I wanted to lick. So I did. I bent over and licked my way down his abs, humming along the ridges of his muscles. He groaned again, and when I undid the top of his jeans, he stilled for just a moment. I looked up at him, and blew cool air over his skin, and watched as his nipples hardened.

I was already so wet for him, and I knew that we shouldn't be doing this. That this would take us down a path that was just going to hurt both of us, but I didn't care.

I undid the rest of his jeans and slid my hand underneath his boxer briefs. He groaned when I wrapped my fingers around his girth, and my entire body shook.

He was so thick and long, and when I freed him from the confinements of his boxer briefs, I licked my lips and pumped him once, twice, before I swallowed the head of his cock into my mouth.

He slid his hand through my hair, and I groaned again, humming along his length as I sucked him down. His hips began to move, just softly enough that I knew I was the one still in control, even as I hollowed my mouth and let him slide deeper down my throat. He fucked my mouth slowly, and I cupped his balls, rolling them in my hand as I kept going down on him. When he stiffened, I hollowed my cheeks, humming along him, and he pulled away, growling.

Before I knew it, his mouth was on mine, his hand on the back of my neck as he kept me steady. I felt safe, cared for, and I couldn't think about anything else.

He was who I wanted, even if I shouldn't.

And then my shirt was off, and my jeans were being tugged down my legs. I was naked, laying on the table, and his head was between my legs as he slowly licked at my pussy, eating me out until I knew I was going to come at any minute. He sucked on my clit, spearing me with two fingers, and I shook, so close to the edge that I knew just one more lick and I'd fall into the abyss. And then I looked down at him, as he looked up at me, and when our gazes connected, I came. He hummed along my cunt, and I came on his face, my nipples hard, my whole body flushing and shaking.

Then he was over me, kissing me, and I was licking at his lips.

"I'm clean, and we both know you don't need a condom."

He froze, and then he smiled wide before he bit my lip. "I'm clean, too. I promise."

"I trust you, Benjamin," I whispered.

Then he was between my legs, and there was nothing else.

He slid deep, inch by achingly slow inch, filling me. I could feel the heat of him, bare and thick.

"Oh dear God, you're like heaven."

He muttered against my neck, and I knew he was fighting for control just like I was.

"I need you to move," I whispered.

"I'm going to need a fucking minute. You're way too fucking hot."

I grinned, even as I shook again.

When he moved, I wrapped my legs around him, groaning when he pumped into me, keeping my hips down onto the table, both of us arching for one another. I came again, clamping around his cock, and he cursed under his breath before muttering my name. He filled me up, and I could feel the heat of him as he spurted into me.

His cock twitched, and my body clenched around him. We both clung to one another, sweaty and shaking, and he looked down at me.

"We're not very good at being friends, are we?" He whispered as he kissed me again. I looked up at him and brushed my fingers along his cheek.

"I don't think we were meant to be just friends, not with the choices that we made." It was the most honest thing I had ever said, and I was afraid that I'd buried myself within more than just what we had begun now. I wasn't sure what I wanted, yet I knew that Benjamin needed to be part of it. Yes, this could be a mistake, but it felt like this was meant to be.

And it might be wrong, but I wasn't sure what else I was supposed to do or say. Or who I was supposed to be.

"Are you okay?" he asked softly.

"I am," I said, needing to touch him. I slid my hands up and down his chest, and he kept touching me, even as I lay on the hard table, his softening cock still deep inside me.

"We'll figure it out. You and me. Together."

I knew he was saying the words that he needed to say and the ones I wanted to hear, and I wanted this to be true, because one drunken night before hadn't been a mistake, but it *had* been a choice.

Tonight had been a completely different choice, one that could ruin everything, or be the start of something I had never allowed myself to believe or give into.

He kissed me again, and I didn't care about the consequences.

Even if I knew I might regret that thought the moment I let myself breathe.

CHAPTER FIFTEEN

Benjamin

I frowned as I went over my schedule for the next day and sipped my coffee. I had two consults with the rest of the family and then another consult by myself. That would take most of the day, and I wasn't even sure when I would be able to get my hands dirty. That was understandable, though, because sometimes my job as the boss of this arm of Montgomery Builders meant that I couldn't do what I thought I was good at. Instead, I got to work on paperwork while my team got to dig in the dirt.

Someone knocked on the door, pulling me from my thoughts. I frowned, taking my coffee with me as I made my way over.

I looked through the peephole and sighed as I opened the door.

"Hello, I didn't realize you were here. Going to punch me again?"

Beckett winced as he walked in, Lee behind him.

"No punching needed," Lee stated as he stared at my coffee. "Do you have more of that?" he asked, sounding practically giddy.

"I do. It's in the kitchen. Help yourself to some."

"Is that sarcasm?" Lee asked, winking, and I rolled my eyes. "Not sarcasm, just being polite since you're in my home."

"I'm sorry," Beckett muttered as he poured himself a cup of coffee and did the same for Lee.

My brows shot up, and I met Lee's gaze.

Lee shrugged. "It's been a long morning." Lee took the coffee cup from Beckett and sighed deeply into it. "Mm, are these the beans Brenna gave you?" he asked, not so innocently.

I narrowed my gaze. "Yes. Got a problem with that?"

"I see you're defensive," Lee sighed. "However, not with me. It's probably the twin next to me."

"I'm an idiot," Beckett said, and I shrugged and took a sip of my coffee. "Not going to say you're not, because, well, you are. I guess so am I."

Beckett rolled his eyes. "I was just so shocked, and honestly? With the way I treated Brenna before, I think I conflated the two in my head. I shouldn't have tried to hit you."

I shrugged. "I'm not going to get in the way of you and Brenna."

"There is no me and Brenna. We're just friends."

"I know that, but I'm still going to get growly. Sue me."

"I can't believe that you guys are having a kid." Beckett shook his head. "It's just so out of the blue."

"I know, but we're making it work. Somehow. We talked about the whole childcare aspect and work, but we haven't gotten into everything else."

"Like where you'll live or if you're dating?" Lee asked, raising a brow.

I swallowed another sip of coffee, and Beckett and Lee glanced at one another.

Beckett cursed under his breath, pulled out a ten-dollar bill, and handed it over to Lee.

I looked between the two of them. "What was that for?"

"I figured you two would get together, while Beckett thought that you would take your time and do your quiet, introspective thing while you told yourself you shouldn't be with Brenna even though you two make sense."

I set down my coffee. "What?"

"You two, you clearly slept together again, and now you're working things out. This is going to be interesting—I kind of like the idea of it. I see the way she looks at you and the way that you look at her. I don't know why it took me so long to piece it all together."

I looked at my brother and then at Lee, who was still spouting off random shit that didn't make sense to me.

"We're not. I mean, I don't know what we're doing."

"Well, you'd better figure it out before that kid comes along, or you're going to fuck things up." Beckett winced.

Lee snorted. "This is coming from a man who nearly fucked things up with Eliza when things surprised us both, so I think you should take that with a grain of salt."

"And this is coming from a man who has no plans to get serious with anyone anytime soon or ever." Beckett shook his head.

Lee winked. "You and Brenna? You're going to have a life together. It's going to be something that you can't just walk away from. However, you two fit. You're both quiet sometimes and growly other times. You guys have been friends as long as all of us have, except for the actual Montgomerys. We all joke that Beckett and Brenna are the best of friends, and maybe that used to be the case, but now we've all jumbled together in this group that hangs out as one. You're sleeping with her, and you're all tongue-tied, so that means you have some feelings for her. You wouldn't be sleeping with her and complicating the situation if you didn't."

I set both hands down on the kitchen island and closed my eyes, letting out a breath. "I like her. I always have. It's probably a mistake, but I can't help it."

"Just don't hurt each other," Beckett whispered.

My gaze shot to his. "I don't want that to happen."

"Do your best not to screw it up. Which is pretty much the advice everybody gave me when it came to Eliza."

I snorted. "Don't screw up. I can try that."

"Good. Are you heading over there today? Going to make more plans, or are you going to wing it? Because winging it in this family is starting to work," Lee said as he took another sip of his coffee. "Damn, I'm going to need to ask Brenna about her bean distributor. I'm a little jealous of this coffee."

"How much coffee have you had?" I asked, narrowing my eyes at Lee.

"Too much. My deadline is kicking my ass, but it's fine. I kind of like the fact that all of you guys are settling down. I'm the last one standing."

"You do realize that that's the perfect thing to say before you fall?" Beckett asked.

"Hey, I didn't say I was falling," I sputtered.

Lee and Beckett gave each other a look before they raised their brows at me.

I threw up my hands. "Seriously. I'm not falling. It's way too soon for that. We're just taking it slow."

"You guys are having a baby. I don't think slow is what you're doing," Lee corrected.

"Those are two separate things. Our relationship, and the baby."

"Do you hear yourself right now?" Beckett asked, tilting his head. "Do you hear the nonsense slipping through your lips? You can't separate the two, and you know that. You're just saying that you want the two separated because you're afraid to fuck it up. I get it. It's scary, but you can't separate the two. So, while you say that you're taking it slow and you're not going to complicate your situation, it is complicated. Every adult relationship is, you're just throwing in more wrenches than usual."

"You're saying that Brenna and I shouldn't sleep together again?" I asked, my stomach tightening.

Because maybe that would be the answer. If we fucked this up and decided that we weren't working, we couldn't just walk away. Then again, would we ever have? Our lives were so entangled because of our friendship and families, walking away wouldn't have been an option before. Let alone now, with the baby.

I rubbed my temples, and Lee sighed. "And now he's getting it."

"I got it before. I just ignored it."

"No, you didn't. I know you didn't."

I looked up at Beckett. "I don't want to fuck this up."

"Then don't. I'm not going to tell you what to do because I don't have any answers for you. I love you. You're my fucking twin. My other half that's not my actual other half," he said with a laugh.

"I guess other halves don't work when you're getting married, and I'm, well, with Brenna."

"Good. You've made the first cognitive leap," Lee added. "You're with Brenna. Now think about what your feelings are towards Brenna. I know, it's me saying this. Feelings? Relationships? Commitment? Shudder, shudder, shudder. However, make a choice. Figure out what she wants. And remember that we're here for you. Maybe just to confuse you further, but we are here."

They changed the subject to work, and wedding

plans, even though we didn't get into it too deeply, and I forced myself to think. At least about the topics at hand and not about Brenna.

I was heading over there later today to work on her garden while she was at work. We had planned it. It was something that I had always done as her friend. Now we weren't friends anymore. Not that way.

We kept trying to put things into boxes, as if those labels would make sense and make things easier.

I had a feeling all it was doing was complicating the situation.

By the time we finished our coffees, and the guys headed out, I was more confused than ever, and yet I knew if I just focused on what was in front of me, I would be fine. It was what I did. The rest of my siblings were the ones who panicked or needed to run full steam ahead into whatever situation they were in to fix it. I was the one that sat back and pieced things together to make my choices. The idea that I wasn't right then told me that maybe I did need to breathe a bit more and focus on what I had and what I didn't.

Brenna wasn't home by the time I got to her house, but that was fine. I might not have a key to her place, just like she didn't have a key to mine, as we weren't there yet, but I had everything I needed in my truck. I had to weed out a few things, and I had a plant in the back of my truck that I was going to plant for her.

She had always wanted a bottlebrush in the front of her house but hadn't had time to figure out where it should go. Well, I had the time, and here I was.

I got to get digging, knowing where I wanted to put it and where Brenna would want it as well. She knew I was coming over but didn't know about the bottle-brush. That was fine with me because I wanted to surprise her. This was something she wanted and something I could help with. I might not have any answers for anything else we were doing, but this I could do.

I was just getting the hose out to water the newly planted mini tree when Brenna pulled into the driveway and parked beside me. She'd opened the garage door but didn't bother to park inside. Instead, she got out, her eyes wide. "You said you were going to work on the garden a bit, but I didn't know you'd be doing all this. Is that a bottlebrush? For me?" She clapped her hands together and came over to me before she threw herself into my arms. I dropped the hose and gathered her close, laughing as I held her.

"I'm covered in dirt." I looked down at her. "And you are covered in flour and frosting. It's an interesting mix." I kissed her hard on the mouth, and she sank into me, and it felt right. As if we had been doing this for years rather than just these few moments.

"It's beautiful. Thank you. You know I could have helped you with it though, pick the plant out." She put her hands on her hips, looked around. "It's what I would've chosen, as you know, and yet I could have helped. You didn't need to do everything on your own."

I rolled my eyes, picked up the hose again, and began watering the new plants. "You know that's what I say to you. You don't need to do everything on your own."

"I don't. Seriously. Right?"

"It's nice to do things for you. That it feels like you could use help with things. So just take this as a gift, and take a look at the new beauty."

"It's gorgeous, Benjamin. Thank you." She looked down at herself, and then me. "We are a complete mess."

"Pretty much. I was almost done and was going to head home and shower."

She bit her lip, then looked down my body again. I could practically feel the heat off her gaze. "What do you say we shower here? And we make something to eat for dinner? Maybe we can come up with some plans."

I didn't want to let it bother me that the excuse she

would use for the two of us being together was plans alone. As if we couldn't just be with one another without having to have an excuse. Or maybe I was just thinking too hard.

"You know what, a shower would be nice. And dinner."

"Perfect," she said, and gestured towards the garage. "I'm going to go bring a few things inside. Do you need help out here?"

"I've got it," I answered, shaking my head. "I'll see you in a second."

She bit her lip, smiled at me, and then walked inside.

I wasn't grumpy, but I was overthinking things. I needed to take things as they came and not to make trouble where there wasn't. That's what my brothers would say, so that was what I would do.

I finished watering the plants, put away my tools, and walked into the house through the garage. Brenna was nowhere to be seen, but I heard her singing to herself from the back of the house. She sounded better than she had, and she had told me this morning that she had been able to keep some of the soup down from the night before.

I had to count that as progress because I didn't like seeing her sick.

I followed her voice, wondering if the shower invite had been a true invite or just an instruction.

Brenna was in the bathroom, just stripping off her shirt when I walked in. She froze, her hands above her head, her lace-clad breasts right there in front of me, and I couldn't help but look.

"I wasn't very clear earlier about the whole shower thing."

I met her gaze. "We need to get clean," I teased, not thinking about anything serious. That would just make things too complicated.

Even though the voice in the back of my head told me they were complicated. But we were just playing pretend at this point. At least that's what it felt like.

And I didn't want to think anymore. Thinking hurt, and I was afraid of what I would come up with if I truly let myself get through everything in my head.

I moved forward and gently pulled the shirt off her arms up over my head, brushed my lips to hers, and she groaned, wrapping her body around me.

"You are dirty."

"And you taste like frosting," I muttered. I bit her lip, and she groaned.

"Keeping things down?"

Smooth, Benjamin. Smooth.

She made a face. "Yes, but that's not sexy talk."

"Not everything that we talk about has to be sexy, Brenna." I didn't know why I was harping on this, and when she gave me a weird look, I pushed that aside.

"Sorry, but are you keeping things down?"

"For twenty-four hours so far. I'm counting that as a win. Now, I seriously need a shower."

"We can do that."

I reached around her into the shower and turned on the hot water before I stripped off my shirt over my head.

She swallowed hard, her gaze going down my body. I loved how she looked at me when she looked at my chest, or anywhere on me. She always had such a hunger in her gaze that she did her best to quell, but there was no hiding it.

Just like I knew there was no hiding the need on my face.

I kissed her again, not wanting to focus on that, and the two of us took our time stripping one another before we stepped into the shower. I put my back to the spray, protecting her, as she kissed me, her hands going between us. She gripped my cock, squeezing slightly, and I let out a moan. "You keep doing that, and I'm not going to last very long."

"I think you'd be surprised." Then she went to her knees, and I sighed. I slid my hand through her hair, the water slicing over us as she wrapped her plump lips around my dick.

She hummed along my length and I moaned, doing my best not to move. If I did, I'd go too hard too fast, and I'd fuck her mouth until I came, spilling my seed all over those pretty breasts of hers. And of course, that image nearly had me coming, so I pulled away and tugged her up so I could press my lips to hers.

"I wasn't done yet," she complained.

"I'm going to fuck that pretty mouth soon. I'm going to come down that throat of yours and all over your tits. And you're going to fucking like it, but first, I'm going to need to lick that pussy of yours."

Her eyes widened a bit at my dirty talk, but she didn't say anything. Instead, she stepped back slowly to the seat built into the wall, spread her legs for me, and held her knees wide. "Like what you see?" she asked, and I grinned.

"Fuck yeah," I said, before I went to my knees, latching onto her pussy. She tasted of sweet cream and bliss. I spread her folds, opening her more to my gaze. She shuddered in my hold, the water still pounding down around us as she kept her legs wide for me. I pressed her thighs even wider before I delved between her lower lips, sucking at her clit, and pushing my tongue deep inside. She shuddered, whispering my name, and I nearly came at the sound.

I wanted her to scream my name. I wanted to feel her around my dick. I wanted it all.

Only I needed to take my time.

I kept kissing her, sucking up her sweetness before she froze for an instant, and she broke. She was beautiful when she came, her body flushing, her nipples hardening into tight little points. I looked up at her as I sucked down her orgasm, needing to send her nearer to the crest again.

Then she tugged on my shoulders, and I obliged, standing so I could get closer to her.

It took maneuvering, but I lifted her up, grateful for the non-skid in the shower, pressed her back to the wall, and speared her in one thrust. Hot water fell down around us, keeping us wet and slippery and turning me on even more. She dug her nails into my back, calling out my name as I fucked her hard into the shower wall. Her pussy clamped around my dick, and I tightened my jaw, my hands digging bruises into her thighs as I fucked her hard.

When she came again, I couldn't help it. I spilled into her, groaning her name as I took her mouth with mine. My dick twitched as I pumped into her, my orgasm hard and long, as she panted, both of us shaking.

What felt like forever, and also no time at all passed, and then she was kissing me, pushing my hair back from my face in the shower.

"I think we're clean," she whispered, and I snorted.

"No, I think I'm going to have to soap you up," I whispered, keeping her still against that wall. "I can't wait to wash those pretty breasts of yours."

She rolled her eyes. "You just had your mouth on my pussy, and suddenly you want my breasts too?"

"I want everything, Brenna."

I hadn't meant to say that.

Her eyes widened marginally, and the water grew colder. "What are we doing?" she asked, and I knew this wasn't about the shower.

I swallowed hard. "I don't know."

The truth was, I had no idea what we were doing.

I didn't want to stop, even if it was a mistake.

CHAPTER SIXTEEN

Brenna

I scowled, looking down at the cupcakes in front of me. Pink lemonade with a lemon cream cheese frosting and a lemon curd center. They were perfection and what Annabelle had asked for. Only, something was off about them.

I tilted my head and studied them more. I knew that Annabelle would probably want sprinkles. I love sprinkles; they were a decoration perfect for most things, but I didn't have the right ones at home. They were at the bakery, and I wasn't going to drive there on my day off, just for sprinkles for Annabelle.

Okay, I would typically have, but the girls would be here any moment, and I didn't want to be late.

I snapped my fingers and then went to my pantry and picked out the little yellow balls that would be perfect for the top. They were just sugar paste, but they would be the right texture for what I was looking for. They weren't lemon-flavored, nor would they give you that crunch, but it would work.

I just finished decorating them when the doorbell rang, and I smiled. It had been a while since we had a girls' night—not that it was night. We were doing a quick lunch before my doctor's appointment, but this was the time that we had, and we were going to make it work.

I wiped my hands on my apron, took the apron off, and made my way to the front door. On the other side, Paige and Annabelle were already there, with Eliza pulling in behind them.

"You guys are disturbingly always on time."

Paige snorted. "I drove us since Annabelle's been queasy for part of the drive, and she didn't want to drive."

I quickly moved back, letting them in. "What's wrong? Are you okay?"

"I'm getting the second trimester morning sickness? I'm not a fan of how many weeks I'm along, and now it's hitting me."

I rubbed her back in sympathy and pretty much pushed her down onto the couch. "As someone who has to take meds now for my nausea, I understand."

"Is someone sick?" Eliza asked, closing the door behind her. "I made cucumber sandwiches, but they're not cucumber, more like a variety of different kinds of sandwiches, but they're so cute. I like calling them that."

"We always call them tea sandwiches," Paige said as she ran her hand down her sister's back. "Oh, I also brought a couple of side dishes I made—just a few little salads."

My eyes widened. "A few?"

"I wasn't sure what you all could eat. I mean, we have two pregnant women in the group now. That means sometimes they might not want chicken or tuna?"

My hand went to my belly without thought. "No, I'm doing okay right now as long as I take my meds. Before, I could only eat sugar."

"That would be a way to enjoy the day."

"For today, I can do mayonnaise, but I'm not sure about tomorrow. We're going to have to play it by ear."

Annabelle cringed and rubbed her belly. "I swear,

I'm getting as big as a house. I may be having twins, but I didn't realize I would get this big so quickly."

Eliza practically beamed as she went over to her friend, kissed the top of her head, then put her hands on Annabelle's stomach. When it was the group of us, we were comfortable invading each other's space. Out in public, we were a little more careful since we didn't want to invite anyone else to touch us without permission. "I am so happy. My family is all having babies. And you are having a baby soon, too."

I looked over at Eliza and smiled. "Today's the sonogram."

"Is Benjamin meeting you there?" Eliza asked as she helped me set up the rest of the food on the table.

"He is. He has work that he can't miss since it's that time of year."

Annabelle smiled. "I'm glad he's going to be there. Jacob is always there for my appointments."

I shrugged, pushing down any feelings I might have for Benjamin because it wasn't safe to think too hard. "Of course he's going to be there. He's the father."

"And your boyfriend," Paige put in, and Eliza and Annabelle shared a look.

I sighed. "He is my Benjamin. Let's leave it at that."

"Oh, we're absolutely not going to leave it like that," Annabelle teased. "You are having a baby with my brother. We are going to be the aunts of your baby."

Eliza beamed. "All of us will be the aunties of your babies. I'm really excited about this because this is going to give me so much practice for when Beckett and I start the adoption process."

"You're working on that quickly then?" I asked, handing over sparkling water for everybody.

"We're working through the paperwork. It's not going to be easy, but it's what we want."

"Anything you need from us, we're here for you." Paige clapped her hands. "I mean, look at us. I can't believe how grown up we're being. We're having a brunch with pink cupcakes and sparkling water and cider, and no booze because half of us are pregnant."

"And it's ten a.m., and I'm not in the mood to drink," Eliza added dryly.

"Ten a.m. means mimosas," Paige teased.

"That is true. I think I miss mimosas most of all." Annabelle grinned at me.

I snorted. "Mimosas are just so nice. Much nicer than morning sickness, or rather, afternoon sickness."

"All day sickness," Annabelle agreed.

"On that note, let's eat some tuna fish and cupcakes," Paige cheered.

Annabelle groaned. "I am starving, so I'm struggling to eat that, but let's not talk about exactly what we're eating."

"That's fine. We can talk about what your intentions are with our brother," Paige said, rolling her shoulders back, but there was laughter in her gaze.

I swallowed hard. "I intend to co-parent with Benjamin and try not to stress the fuck out because we are still way early into our relationship even though we went about things in an opposite way. Please don't ask me how I feel about him because I don't know, and I don't want to stress out. Can we talk about, maybe, Jacob? Yes, let's talk about Jacob. Or Archer. Archer's getting married. Let's talk about that." Again, Annabelle and Eliza met gazes, and I growled. "What is with that look?"

"It's not a look, more of a question of what to say because it's like you have two different relationships together," Annabelle explained.

"What do you mean?"

Eliza sighed. "On one hand, you guys are discussing co-parenting because you're trying to be adults and not step on each other's toes because you're having a baby. On the other, you're in this new relationship where you're starting to learn one another differently, and putting those together is difficult. You guys are going through this so well, and I love it for you, but if you need to explode, or talk to us, we're here."

I swallowed hard, wondering how I could have thought they wouldn't have seen where I was standing. They were far too observant when it came to their friends. Hell, I was usually on the other side of that aisle.

"We don't want to pry." Paige grimaced. "I mean, we do want to pry because we love you, and he's our family, and you're our family, and we want to know everything. As someone who is also in a relationship, like everybody else here, sometimes we don't have answers. And that's okay that you don't have answers. Do your thing. We're excited for you."

"I love you guys too. Now let's talk about Archer and Marc. Are we throwing them an engagement party?"

"We will allow this change of conversation because, yes, we are throwing Archer an engagement party." Annabelle picked up her phone. "Archer has already talked to us about a few things, and I'm excited for him. Our baby brother's getting married."

"Everybody's changing and growing up. I love it." Paige clapped her hands.

"I wish Archer would have been able to come today. Then we could start planning," I added.

Paige smiled. "He can come next time, and we'll make a huge plan because you know he'll want to go big."

"Does Marc want that?" Eliza asked as she bit into a tea sandwich.

Annabelle nodded. "I think so. Archer said that Marc told him that whatever Archer wants is going to happen."

I met Annabelle's gaze. "They seem nice together."

"They do. Marc is just a lot more reserved than anyone I ever thought would be with Archer."

"It's hard for people to marry into the Montgomerys," Paige muttered.

I had to wonder why it was her saying that and not Eliza and me. Then again, I wasn't getting married, and Paige was the one bringing somebody else into the family, even if they weren't engaged yet.

We talked about a few ideas for Archer, and then baby showers, and work and life and TV and just everything. It was a wonderful lunch, and by the time they left, I was exhausted. Yet energy shot through because I was on my way to my sonogram. I quickly got ready and headed towards my OB, nervous as hell.

Normally I wouldn't have told the Montgomerys about the pregnancy so quickly. I was only nine weeks along, and that wasn't enough time for most people to feel comfortable doing so. I had needed to tell Benjamin, and we hadn't wanted to keep secrets, so that meant we were doing things out of order. That was the label on my relationship with Benjamin. Completely deformed and out of order.

I pulled into the parking lot, and Benjamin was already standing outside, looking down at his phone as he typed quickly. I got my bag and made my way to him. He looked up at me then, his eyes warming for just a second.

My stomach clenched as I looked up at him, and I knew I was in trouble. Just that one look, and I was gone. Damn it, I needed to hold back, rein it in, and yet possibly we're not letting that happen.

"I got here a bit early since I finished up at one location, but I need to head to the other job right after this. Water main break and the next neighborhood is screwing things up for us." He leaned down and kissed me softly. "You look pretty. And taste like mint and lemon?"

"I brushed my teeth after I had a pink lemonade cupcake." I did my best to ignore the flutters in my stomach.

His eyes widened. "Please tell me you saved me some."

That made me smile. "Of course, I did. I'm not going

to make a cupcake you enjoy and hand them all out without giving you one."

"You know, this is why I like you," he teased as we moved towards the front door.

He led us in, and we didn't have to wait long as we were right on time for my appointment. I got awkwardly into the gown and dangled my feet over the end of the bed while Benjamin kept looking at his phone, frowning.

"What's wrong?"

"Work things. And I was trying to give you some privacy while I stood here in the corner and pretended that I wasn't watching you get into a paper gown."

"Yes, because this is the hardest thing you've ever seen." My dry tone made his eyes light up.

"Hey, you're naked under there. I can't help it."

"Benjamin," I scolded as my OB came in.

"Hi there, Brenna, it's good to see you," she said as she walked in.

"Hi, Dr. Geller. This is Benjamin. The um, father." I wasn't good at labels, apparently, but from the look on Benjamin's face, he didn't mind.

"Hello, Benjamin, it's nice to meet you too."

"I'm excited to be here," he said, and it sounded like the truth.

"Good to hear. Since he's here, I'm going to go over

everything with both of you guys, and then we're going to work on the sonogram."

"Okay." There were the normal questions, and at one point, nerves wrecked me, not because it was scary, just because this was different. I was finally doing it. I was going to be a mom.

In the most unexpected of ways.

Benjamin took my hand as the nurse walked in, and we began the sonogram.

I held my breath and tried to look at the screen, wondering what I was seeing. Then the most wonderful sound filled my ears.

A heartbeat. Quick, beautiful, and ours.

"There we go, your baby has a beautiful heartbeat. Everything looks great. I'm going to take a few pictures, and we're going to go over a few more things, but everything looks great for now. Congratulations, you two."

I looked up at Benjamin, and he held my hand tight, his eyes watery. I knew I was crying, and when he leaned down to kiss my cheeks, taking the tears away, I cried even harder.

"We are having a baby," I whispered.

"We are."

I looked up at him, and I knew I was in trouble. So damn in trouble. Because I couldn't fall for him. Not so quickly. I couldn't want more when we were figuring out what we had right then.

I was falling. Far too quickly, far too hard.

I knew when it came to the Montgomerys, once you fell, there was no getting back up. You were lost. Only I wasn't sure he would fall with me, as that wasn't the promise we had made. I was falling in love with Benjamin Montgomery, a single mistake I knew could break everything.

CHAPTER SEVENTEEN

Benjamin

"Is this our first date?" Brenna asked me.

I looked up at her over the menu. "Considering we're having a baby and spend most days together while we're not working, I don't know if this can constitute a first date."

She scrunched up her nose before she shook her head, a smile finally playing on her face. I looked around at Colton's restaurant; I had been here a few times before. There was good food and a pleasant atmosphere, and it wasn't too fancy for our taste, nor was it a hole in the wall with greasy food.

It had been a long few weeks between our jobs and trying to figure out a regular routine. We slept at each other's houses more often than not, and it felt as if we had fallen into a serious relationship right away, rather than working our way up to it. The thing was, I didn't mind. I liked what we were doing. It felt as if time made sense, that this is what we should have been doing this entire time.

That wasn't the right way to think and maybe that would only confuse things in the end, but I wasn't sure.

I had never expected Brenna, but I wanted to know more. I had always liked her, always loved her, just in a different way. She was my friend, the one that made me smile and laugh. She was always there for me no matter what, and I knew I did my best to be the same for her. Only things were different now, and I knew she kept us at arm's length for a reason. If we broke up or broke off whatever the hell we were doing, things would be difficult for both of us. For the baby. I didn't want this to end. I wanted more.

I wasn't sure when that had happened.

"I'm starving. I think I could eat half of this menu."

I looked up at her and grinned. "You want to get two big meals and share? Then there will be leftovers."

"That sounds like a plan. Although, I'm suddenly

craving salmon even though I haven't wanted salmon in years, and I think it's because I can't have it."

"I won't tell you about the cheese plate I thought about getting then," I said with a grimace.

She narrowed her eyes at me. "Do not talk about soft cheeses in front of me. That's not very nice."

I snorted as the waiter came to take our orders.

Colton was in the back of the restaurant and had come out when we had first shown up. I liked the guy and thought he was good for Paige, but I knew Paige was getting antsy, and so I wanted to know what his intentions were with my baby sister.

Brenna laughed suddenly, and I looked over at her. "What?"

"I can just picture you right now imagining walking back into the kitchen and asking Colton to declare his intentions for Paige."

"How the hell did you read my mind like that?"

"Because I know you, Benjamin. It's sort of what you do."

"I just don't know if I like the fact that I don't know Colton, or even Marc for that matter, as much as I do Jacob," I said after a moment.

"Do you try?" she asked, tilting her head.

"I do. They don't hang out with us as much. I get it, we're a lot to deal with, and we all have lives, but we're needy. And protective. I know you're shocked at that revelation."

She rolled her eyes. "Completely shocked. I guess Eliza got off easy because she already was well ensconced in the Montgomerys to begin with."

"And you too."

Her eyes widened. "Yes. Me too."

The way she said that made me think she still didn't think of herself as mine, as someone connected to the Montgomerys through a relationship.

I wasn't sure what to think about that. Or even if I should feel too much about that. Damn it, I was falling for her. I wanted her in my life, and she was going to be the mother of my child, but what if I wanted more?

And I didn't know if she was going to let that happen.

We talked about less serious stuff over dinner, and then about upcoming doctor's appointments.

By the end of the meal, when I was full and we were waiting on our check, Brenna pulled out the sonogram.

"So the next one, we should be able to see a little more resolution, right?" she asked as she looked down at the black and white image. I swallowed hard and tapped it.

"Your insurance covers the 4D one, right?"

"Yes, but not for a little while. I have to be further

along. That's just going to be so weird. I know we saw Annabelle and Jacob's, and you saw those two little faces, but it feels real when you look at that. Instead of a blob."

I snorted. "Yes, it will be a little weird not just seeing a blob. Of course, I used to think babies looked like little aliens until they were around two months old."

Brenna snorted. "Oh my God, me too. I know people say babies are cute, but not all of them. It takes a while for them to grow into cute. And if you ever tell our friends and family that I said that, I will murder you."

"Between all of your nieces and nephews, you must have held a lot of babies."

"My fair share. I need to head out there again soon since my sister's about to give birth any minute now."

"You missed the birth of your brother's kid, right?" I asked, frowning.

Brenna bit her lip, sighed. "Yes, but I'm trying my best to make it to this one. It's going to get a little more complicated when I'm further along, but with all of my family seemingly having babies one after another, I can't take as much time off as I would like to since they live on the other side of the country."

"Do you want me to come with you?" I asked, my voice low.

She blinked and swallowed hard. "You're welcome to. I mean, you've already been there, and they know you, and you did get me knocked up, so they might have questions," she muttered.

I snorted. "I got the phone call from your brother, your father, and your sisters. Don't worry. They had questions."

"I still can't believe they did that."

"Of course you believe it. It's what they do, just like my family. But they weren't rude about it. Just posturing."

She shook her head as the waitress came with the check. Her eyes widened as she looked at the sonogram and grinned at the two of us. "Oh, you guys, I'm so happy for you. I didn't even realize when you had gotten married. Colton hadn't mentioned it. Congratulations. So many babies in the Montgomerys. That's wonderful." She tapped the check on the table, and grinned, and walked away, leaving me shaken.

"I hadn't realized she had known you were a Montgomery," Brenna said, her voice soft.

I swallowed hard, took out cash so we wouldn't have to wait for the credit card to process, and grabbed the bag of leftovers. "Come on. We'll head out of here."

"What? Oh, that sounds good. Sure."

I held back a curse, knowing that when someone

thought we were married or had questions about our future, Brenna took two steps back.

I didn't know when I became the one to think of our relationship as something that needed to move forward, but I was. I was there, and I wanted more. That meant I needed more from Brenna. I just wasn't sure how to ask her to make that happen.

She was quiet on the car ride back to her place, where I thought I would be spending the night, but after the way she kept looking at me and frowning, I wasn't sure I would be welcome. She was going to do her best to push me away again. I didn't know why. Things were working, but maybe I wasn't what she wanted.

I needed to talk to her tell her what I was thinking. Why did that sound so much easier on paper than it did when it was real life?

I pulled into her driveway and picked up the take-out. Without another word, we walked inside through the garage.

"Benjamin, we need to talk."

I held back a curse, knowing what was coming. "I should put the food in the refrigerator, so it doesn't go bad."

"Okay. This feels so domestic."

I shook my head, stuffing the bag in the fridge

without really caring where it went. "Of course, it looks domestic. We're having a kid. I'm in your house. That's domestic."

"I don't want to confuse the baby."

I swallowed hard, knowing where she was going with this. Frankly, I was surprised it hadn't come up sooner, or that it wasn't me saying it. "Confuse the baby? Or you."

"Maybe that's it, too. I don't know. But maybe we should stop. Take a step back and realize where we are."

"Just like that?"

"Maybe it'd be best."

"Best for who? For you? Should we have defined labels? Because I wouldn't mind that. I wouldn't mind knowing who we are or what we want from each other. We weren't in the same position when we slept together, nor are we in the same position when we found out we were pregnant. Things are different now. You can feel it."

"I know things are different, but it's just happening so quickly. I don't want you to wake up one day and realize that you were forced into this."

"Brenna. Frankly, I'm doing my best not to scare you, but this is reality. Not some movie."

She nodded, swallowing hard. "I know that. If it were some movie, I'd end up falling for my best friend like everyone else thought, not his twin where everybody gets confused, and I don't know what I'm doing."

"What the fuck, Brenna?" I asked, ice flooding through my veins.

"That's not what I meant."

"Then why did you bring him up?"

"Because everybody thought I was supposed to be with Beckett, and I didn't want him like that. And suddenly I'm with you, and I want you? I don't know how it happened. And now I'm afraid that people keep pushing us in this direction, and you're not going to want this."

"Stop telling me what I want. I'm trying not to tell you what you want, so you don't get to do the same for me." I paused and blurted, "Am I just his replacement?"

"What the fuck? That's not what I said."

"Then why bring him up?" I asked again.

"Because he's part of this. He's your twin, my best friend. Things are complicated. He doesn't have anything to do with this." She put her hands over her stomach. "Our baby. And I feel like everything's getting confused and going too fast, and I need a moment to breathe."

"I like you, Brenna," I said after a moment. "Fuck it. I'm falling in love with you." Her eyes widened, and I hated myself. "I don't know what I'm supposed to do about it, what we're supposed to do about it. Because you might not have asked for this, but neither did I. But here we are, I'm fucking falling in love with you, and every time I look at you, I'm afraid you're not going to feel the same way."

"I don't know what we're supposed to do, Benjamin. It wasn't supposed to be this way. What if we keep doing this and we realize that we were doing it for the wrong reasons? We'll just hurt each other more. I'm scared."

She swallowed hard, and I cursed. I moved forward, cupping her face. "I don't know what we're going to do, Brenna. We can't run away from each other."

"I don't want to run. I need to think."

She didn't push me away then though, she put her arms around my waist and held me close, and I did the same, inhaling her scent and telling myself that this wasn't an end. That she wasn't pushing me away for good. She was scared, and fuck, so was I, but I was terrified that somehow this wasn't going to be enough. That I wasn't going to be enough. When Brenna got scared, she faced things head-on by taking care of others. Never herself.

I didn't know where I stood in her mind.

Nor did I know what would happen once I let go and finally let myself believe.

CHAPTER EIGHTEEN

Brenna

I wasn't sure I could blame everything on hormones, yet part of me knew that might be the case right now. My body hurt, my soul ached, and I felt like all I did was make mistake after mistake.

I had been so mean to myself and Benjamin the night before. So casually cruel. I knew I was acting off, that I wasn't saying the right things, but as I opened my mouth, random words just tumbled out.

There was no excuse other than I needed to stop and take a minute to think of what I was doing.

"You want to talk about it?" Archer asked me from

my side, and I turned, doing my best to pull myself from my thoughts.

We were at Riggs', doing our best to do monthly evenings at the bar. We used to do it weekly, but between work and new challenges and changes in our lives, we were no longer able to meet up as often. I wasn't sure how I felt about that, as I already missed how much time we had spent with one another. However, maybe it was for the best. After all, I didn't know where I stood with Benjamin, and I knew the others were going to be able to tell that something was off with us the moment they looked at us. Considering Archer was here talking to me about it right then, I had been right.

"Everything's fine," I lied.

"You can't lie to me, Brenna. You're my friend, and having a baby with my brother. I can tell these things."

"Me being pregnant with a Montgomery baby means that suddenly you can read my thoughts?" I asked, teasing, though not fully teasing. I wouldn't be surprised if some radar and tracking software came with the Montgomerys.

"Not that way, though that would be a cool trick," Archer said with a laugh.

I shook my head. "I'm fine. I need to think."

"You can think and talk."

"We are in the middle of the bar while most of the family is on the dance floor, and I don't think that me talking about my problems or lack thereof right now is the best thing."

"Know I'm always here for you like I know you will always be here for me." Something in his tone worried me, but when his face closed off, I realized that maybe I wasn't the only one lost in my feelings and thoughts. I wanted to say something, ask what was wrong, but I couldn't. There was something in his face that told me he wasn't ready to talk about it. Well, I wasn't prepared either. So we made for a pair.

I opened my mouth to say something, but then Benjamin finally walked in. I wasn't going to lie and say I hadn't been looking for him this whole time, because I had. He had been running late with an issue at work, which seemed to be coming up more often than not recently. He was on a tough job that was taking almost all of his time, and while I understood that, I couldn't help but wonder if he was grateful for the reprieve from my awkwardness. Once again, I was centering all of our decisions on myself, and I needed to stop doing that.

"And I see I'm no longer needed in this conversation," Archer teased. I looked over at him.

"What?" I ask, blinking back to the now.

"Oh, nothing. Don't worry about it. However, your

man is here. You should talk to him, tell him how you feel."

I looked at him and then at our crowd of people that did not include his fiancé.

"You want to talk about feelings?" I asked pointedly.

He rolled his eyes. "Marc is out of for business, something you well know. That's why he's not here. He always comes to Montgomery events at Riggs', while I go with him to his business meetings at high-end bars that serve martinis that are more expensive than my first car."

That made me smirk. "You guys are making it work, though."

He smiled, his eyes full of love. "We are. We come from different walks of life, and we don't always agree on everything, but we shouldn't have to. We're allowed to have our own opinions and wants and needs. We compromise with each other, and speaking to one another is what makes a relationship work."

"When did you get so wise, Archer Montgomery?"

"I've always been wise. You have just been too lost in your thoughts to see it."

"Maybe."

"You don't have to make all of your decisions right away. If you aren't ready for something serious beyond having a baby, which—hello—is very serious, make sure he knows that. If you're just scared, and that's why you're walking away or pushing him away? Then make sure you realize that's what it is."

"I didn't tell you a single thing, Archer. Did Benjamin talk to you?" I asked, my heart racing. How could Archer know me so well?

From the look on his face, I knew I had just stepped in it. He had been guessing, fishing, and I had spilled the beans.

"He didn't have to, nor did you."

"It's not like that."

"It's not like anything. Take your time, breathe. And know that you do not need to fall into anyone's timelines but yours, as long as you remember that Benjamin might have his ideas."

Archer kissed me softly on the cheek, and then practically pushed me towards Benjamin.

As soon as I saw Benjamin, though, all thoughts of being rational slid out of my mind. I couldn't think when he was around. And that was a problem. I was the rational one. Not prone to emotional decisions. But every time I was near him, I threw myself into those bad decisions. I didn't want to be this person, but how long could I blame the hormones for this mess?

"Hey," he said as he stepped near me.

I swallowed hard.

"Hi."

"I'm glad you're here. I was afraid you weren't going to come."

He was so quiet. I was so scared. What if I'd let myself fall like he was saying, and it wasn't it? This was a unique situation, and I wasn't sure what we were supposed to do. Why was I making so many mistakes?

"Are you going to talk to me?" Benjamin asked, and I shook my head.

"I should go."

"Brenna," he said, clearly exasperated.

"What?" I barked, my emotions going out of control.

The others were looking at us now, and I knew they probably wanted to say something, but I didn't have the time nor the inclination to deal with it. All I did was screw things up. I was pregnant, having a fucking baby, and I couldn't have a fucking conversation because I was too afraid of what he was going to say. I didn't deserve any happiness that was going to come from him because I was the one that kept screwing things up. I was going to hurt him. I knew it.

I didn't know how to fix it.

"Brenna, we need to talk."

"I should go."

"Are you feeling okay?" he asked, his tone changing on a dime. He wasn't angry with me. No, he was worried. Worried because he loved me? Or he thought he had to?

Why couldn't I think clearly?

"I should go. I'm just making things worse."

I moved forward, and he followed me, muttering over his shoulder to Archer about something. I knew Archer would tell the others that I needed space or something, and I didn't care.

I couldn't think, not at a bar surrounded by people that I loved, and certainly not with a man that I didn't want to love.

Was that it? Did I not want to love him?

That couldn't be it. Was I falling in love with Benjamin Montgomery?

Of course I was. How could I not? What if he figured out that he didn't love me?

I wiped away a tear, pissed off at myself, as I picked up my phone.

"What are you doing?" he asked, coming to my side.

"Archer drove me, so I'm getting a ride share so I can get home."

"You're not getting a fucking ride share. Not now, and certainly not in the rain. I'll take you home."

"I'm fine. You don't need to drop everything and do everything for me. I can do this."

"I'm sure you can. You've always been able to do everything on your own, but you don't have to do this on your own."

"What? Have a baby?"

"That's not what I fucking meant. And you know you're not doing it on your own. You *and* me."

"I should just go and breathe, I need to breathe," I said, after a minute.

"Everything okay out here?" Beckett asked, and I wanted to scream. This is the exact wrong time for this. I was still so angry with Beckett for the way that he had gotten in Benjamin's face before. Beckett had no right to try to stand up for me the way he had. Every time that things got complicated between us, between Benjamin and me, Beckett was there, trying to be my best friend and Benjamin's twin at the same time. It just made everything so weird and challenging.

"I can handle this, Beckett. You should go inside," Benjamin growled, his gaze on mine.

"Brenna?" Beckett asked.

I cursed. "Go inside. Benjamin and I are having a discussion. You don't need to be part of this."

I knew I was being a bitch, but things were touchy

just then, and I didn't know what to do. This was my fault, and I needed to fix it.

Only there wasn't going to be any fixing this if we didn't talk.

Beckett looked between us before giving us a nod and walking back inside. Eliza stood in the doorway and cringed as she tugged Beckett in, a little forcefully if I thought about it.

Benjamin was so silent I was afraid everything was going to blow up in my face right then. "Come on. I'll get you home."

"I'm sorry for ruining the night," I whispered.

He cursed again. "You didn't. We're finally having the conversations that we didn't have before, and things just kept getting fucked up because we're not talking to one another."

"I know. I think it's just hitting me right now that we're having a baby and everything that we said last night, and I need a minute to think. I really shouldn't have come out tonight."

He sighed as we got in the truck. "I shouldn't have come out either, but I didn't want you to be alone."

There it was. Both of us not wanting each other to be alone.

I was in love with him.

I wasn't sure how to tell him. Because if I said it

wrong, then would he think it was the truth? Or just me trying to make things easier?

"I hate that we even brought Beckett up last night." Benjamin gripped the steering wheel, his jaw tight.

"Why would you think that?"

He looked over at me before pulling his gaze back to the road. The roads weren't easy, and the rain was coming down hard. My pulse raced, and I was terrified we were going to say something we would regret.

"What is Beckett going to say?" I asked, knowing it was probably the wrong thing, but Benjamin had brought him up, and now we'd have to deal with it.

He growled. "Seriously? That's what you're going to ask? What the hell does Beckett have to do with this?"

"He has everything to do with things. You can't just pretend that's not a problem."

"Well, maybe if he wasn't at the center of everything, we could have a fucking conversation," he snapped.

I looked at him then, but lights hit the windshield. He narrowed his eyes, trying to see what was going on. We were in our lane, but lights were coming at us fast. I screamed, and then the glass shattered, and metal screeched. I reached for Benjamin.

I caught only air.

Then there was nothing.

CHAPTER NINETEEN

Brenna

I woke up to the sound of my screams, only they were of an echo, not truly what I was doing at that exact moment.

"You're safe, you're safe," a deep voice said next to me. I knew that voice. I loved that voice, but it wasn't the voice I needed to hear.

"Beckett?" I muttered.

"I'm here, Brenna."

"Go get the nurse, Archer."

"I'm on it," Archer whispered as there was a scuffle

of shoes against tile. I tried to think, tried to do anything, but I couldn't.

I opened my eyes, then closed them again, the light hitting me too brightly.

"The baby?" I asked, the first thought to my mind.

"We're not family, so they're not telling us anything. I'm only allowed in here because I'm your emergency contact."

"My phone," I muttered, remembering that I had put him in as my emergency contact in my phone a while ago just in case I had been in an accident. Like this.

"Benjamin," I said quickly, trying to get up from the bed.

The lights nearly blinded me, and everything ached, but Beckett reached out and gripped my hand. "He's in the room next door. He should be fine."

"Should?" I asked, not crying because I couldn't, couldn't do anything. The shock was too real. But everything ached.

"The rest of the family's with him. Mom and Dad too. Archer and I were in here with you."

"What happened?"

"We're not sure, but it looks like a car jumped the median and hit you guys nearly head-on. You weren't going that fast, and even in the rain, you guys were driving safely. It hit you, and the truck's totaled."

"I'm so scared. And they won't tell you about the baby?" My hands went to my stomach, and I held back a sob. I needed to be strong, but all I wanted to do was break.

Beckett shook his head. "No, I don't know anything about what's going on, only that I'm here with you. No matter what."

"I need to see Benjamin," I whispered.

I needed to tell him that I was sorry for overreacting, for being so scared that I had almost lost everything.

"We'll make that happen. You should rest. We can talk later."

"I need to talk to him now. I need him to know."

I needed to tell him that I loved him. I didn't want to tell Beckett that. Beckett didn't need to be the first person to hear those words.

"We'll get him in here, I promise. Just breathe. You need to take care of yourself."

"The doctor's on his way," Archer said, out of breath. "I'm just glad that you're okay. Well, you know."

We didn't know, and that was the problem.

Archer looked between Beckett and me, and nodded

tightly, then headed back out, though I wasn't sure exactly why.

"I'm so sorry," Beckett whispered.

I frowned, looking up at him, my head aching.

"If I hadn't been such a guilty asshole for treating you the way that I did the past few months, I wouldn't feel like I'm one of the reasons that you and Benjamin keep fighting."

"That's not it. I promise you. Benjamin and I have our own issues, but in reality, they have nothing to do with you. I promise."

"I just want you to know that I love you," he whispered.

"I love you too," I sighed. "Just not like that."

Beckett reached for my hand, squeezed it slightly, then looked up and froze. I followed his gaze and blinked.

Benjamin stood in the doorway, in a hospital gown, a bloody bandage on his forehead, and an IV sticking out of his arm as he leaned against the IV pole.

"What the fuck are you doing out of bed?" Beckett growled.

"I needed to see. I needed to make sure she was okay."

"Fuck, come sit down."

"I don't think I can move right now. They kind of pumped me up with a lot of drugs."

I tried to get up, and both twins gave me identical glares, so I sat there, nerves racking me at the thought of what could be wrong with Benjamin, the baby, everything.

Before I could say anything, two harried nurses came in and started trying to move Benjamin around, growling at him.

"I need to make sure that the baby's okay. That Brenna's okay. I know I'm not supposed to be out of bed, but for fuck's sake, just let me see her."

"There's no need for that kind of language, young man," an older nurse said as she walked in, a glare on her face. "If you don't sit down, we'll make you."

"Benjamin, stop being an idiot," Beckett growled, and they shoved Benjamin into the wheelchair behind him.

"I just need to know," he whispered. "I needed to see you." Benjamin turned to me, and my heart broke. He was here, bloody and in pain, but he was alive. And I needed to know about the baby.

The room I was in had two beds, with a curtain separating them. The other bed was empty, and with a few pointed questions, and nurses that I would forever be grateful towards, they put Benjamin in the bed next to me.

Another doctor came in and began talking about ultrasounds and checks, but I couldn't keep up. "We're going to check for a heartbeat, and together we're going to get through this. Now Benjamin, sit still and let the nurses take care of you, or they're not going to let this happen. Do you understand me?"

Her voice was fierce, and we both nodded before Beckett quietly left the room, leaving us with the staff and each other.

The beds were close enough that Benjamin and I could reach out and grip each other's hands, and I squeezed hard, wanting him closer but knowing we couldn't be yet.

The nurses worked on him and me, and then the most beautiful sound in the world reached our ears.

"There it is, the heartbeat. Everything looks good here. I'm going to run a few more tests, but the baby looks good here."

I looked over at Benjamin, and I wept.

CHAPTER TWENTY

Benjamin

I t took over an hour of poking and prodding before they finally left us alone long enough that I could crawl out of bed.

Brenna narrowed her eyes but moved over so I could sit next to her. I no longer had an IV and didn't need any pain meds. I had a slight concussion, was still attached to all the monitors, but only needed a few stitches on my forehead. Brenna needed stitches on her shoulder, as well as right on her cheekbone, and it might scar depending on how it healed, but we would both be fine.

The baby was fine.

I could barely breathe with the relief shooting through me.

"Hey," I whispered as I crawled into her bed and held her close. "Everything's okay."

"The staff is going to get angry at us again," she said.

"Maybe, I don't give a fuck right now. With as much money as the Montgomery's pour into this hospital with how many times we're here? We can hold each other for a minute."

"I'm so sorry," she blurted.

I frowned. "Why are you sorry?"

"If I hadn't gotten scared and pushed you away, we wouldn't have been in the car, and this wouldn't have happened."

I leaned down and kissed her brow, the sounds of her screams still echoing in my head. "Stop it. There was an oil slick on the road, and the other guy was going too fast, especially in the rain. He hit us; it wasn't your fault."

"Is he okay?"

That was my Brenna, worried about the other guy while she had stitches on her face. "He has a broken leg, but he's fine. At least that's what Beckett growled at me."

"If I hadn't wanted to leave, we wouldn't have been in the car. We could have lost the baby."

"We didn't. And I wanted to leave, too. I was only there because I wanted to be with you. I always want to be with you, Brenna. Maybe we didn't go about this the right way, but it's our way." I pause. "I love you, Brenna. You're mine. You and the baby. I love you both. And I know that this isn't going to be easy. Nothing is, but we can find a path that works for us. I don't want to lose you, Brenna."

She reached up, her fingers touching the edge of the bandage. "I almost lost you tonight. I don't want to lose you either."

"I know it might be too soon for you to say anything, for you to get through all of your emotions because I know you keep thinking too hard, but I need to be here. No matter what."

My heart ached, and I wanted her to say the words back, but I knew that she might not be able to. It would be too quick for her, and I understood that.

It didn't ease the wanting, though.

She put her fingers to my lips then and smiled. "I love you too, Benjamin Montgomery. This isn't exactly how I pictured saying it, but maybe it's how it needed to be. I think I started falling in love with you on that road trip when I got to spend time with just you without the others around us. You faced my family, faced my own tumbled thoughts. And you haven't shied away. You haven't run away. I was the one who tried to do the running, and I failed. I love you, Benjamin. And we're making a family."

"We already are a family. We're just growing it. And I can't wait to see what else we do." I leaned down and kissed her and ignored the throat-clearing of a nurse that walked in. Yes, we were going to be in trouble. Yes, if we weren't careful, we'd somehow get kicked out of the hospital, even if I wasn't sure that actually could happen. It didn't matter. I was holding the woman that I loved, the future mother of my child, and nothing else mattered.

CHAPTER TWENTY-ONE

Benjamin

This Montgomery Ink family dinner hit a little different. Probably because there weren't going to be any new announcements from Brenna and me. The family already knew that we were engaged, that we had a child on the way, and we were working on moving her into my house. I had the extra space, and my place was closer to both of our works. It only made sense. We were still trying to figure out if we would sell her place or do what Annabelle and Jacob had done and rent out the house to somebody. Those are decisions that would come soon, but were not the major ones that we had already announced to the family. Today, however, was just about food and wedding planning. Just not ours. No, first up was Beckett and Eliza, Archer and Marc, and then us. I didn't think we were going to go to something too big, not like the others. No, we had talked about just a small backyard wedding, one possibly a little sooner rather than later, since Brenna wasn't sure she wanted to go full Grecian gown over a large baby bump.

I didn't care. As long as Brenna was by my side, that was all that mattered.

I hadn't been expecting her, but I wasn't sure you could expect her. She was full of surprises. With every new breath I took, I felt like I was falling harder for this woman, finding unique aspects about her that I wasn't prepared for.

Part of me thought that perhaps we'd always one day be at this spot, maybe not in this exact way, but we would be together. It might have taken getting my ex-girlfriend pregnant so she could have a baby with her wife to get me here, but that was not the strangest way a family member of mine had fallen in love.

"Why are you smiling like that?" Brenna asked from my side as she wrapped her arm around my waist.

It had been a couple of weeks since the accident, and we were both healed, though the cuts on our faces were going to need a little bit longer before they entirely faded away. One of our cousin's friends was a plastic surgeon and had come in to help with the stitches in the end.

I wasn't sure what it said about the Montgomerys that we had a plastic surgeon on hand for accidents, but I'd do whatever it took to make sure Brenna never had to think about almost losing each other again.

I'd never forget, however, as I dreamed about it often, yet waking up to Brenna in my arms helped.

"I was thinking about weddings and how our families exploded over the past year or so."

She looked up at me and grinned. "You're right. What's funny is I felt like I've always been here. And I have. I've been the best friend of the Montgomerys, and now I'm going to have your last name. That is, if my family lets me change it."

I snorted, thinking about her family, her parents, brothers, and sisters. "Your sisters changed their last name to their husbands'."

"They did, but I was the last holdout. And I think they are afraid the Montgomerys will truly take over the rest of the world."

"It only takes a few more marriages, and then we'll probably have enough of us in offices and leadership roles around the country. First the US, and then the world. Soon it will just be the United States of Montgomerys."

She blinked up at me and burst out laughing. "You sounded so serious just then."

"I am serious. It's in our doctrine. Soon you'll learn it. Once you get the tattoo."

She rolled her eyes. "I've always wanted the Montgomery Ink Iris. Are we going to go down to Denver or Colorado Springs to get it done?" she asked, speaking of the two tattoo shops that were in our family.

"You make the decision, though there will be a battle over who gets to do it."

"Really?"

"Pretty much. I think it's an inside family joke, but Austin Montgomery did mine."

"Then maybe he should do mine too."

"That's a good way to make it work. That way, you don't have to make a decision."

"I like the sound of that," she whispered, and I leaned down and brushed my lips against hers.

"Seriously? Again?" Beckett asked, clearing his throat as he stood beside us.

I looked at my twin and shook my head. "You were just making out with Eliza in the corner."

Eliza giggled from my twin's side. "You caught us," she teased.

"Brenna is my best friend. Just watch where you make out with her," Beckett replied, a little bit of laughter in his gaze.

"I do think that this group is getting a little too close," Lee announced as he walked into the room, staring between all of us. "I think I'm officially the last holdout."

I looked at the only single person in the house and laughed. "Pretty much. Everybody is either married, having children, or in a serious relationship."

Lee took a sip of his beer. "I'm never settling down. You do realize that, right? It's a point of pride at this point."

I met Brenna's gaze, and she snorted. After all, I was pretty sure both of us had said that at one point or another in the past few months.

I looked around at my family and knew that things were going to change again soon. In a few months, there would be babies and then children laughing and jumping around. Weddings and birthday parties, and other events to bring us together.

We hadn't always been good about speaking our thoughts or opening up to one another, not as much as our cousins were with their family. We were getting better at it, though.

Beckett and Eliza grinned at each other, whispering secrets that had nothing to do with us. We were only part of their little world. Annabelle was on the couch while her husband rubbed her ankles. Archer and Marc laughed with my parents, Marc smiling softly as he looked at Archer, while Archer waved his hands wildly as they made plans for their engagement party.

Paige and Colton were on the deck, both of them looking serious, but not like they were fighting, so I didn't say anything. It wasn't my place, at least for now. Of course, as I looked, Beckett also glanced over at the deck and narrowed his gaze.

It seemed that I wasn't the only one ready to stand in and protect our little sister, even if she didn't need any protection.

"Hey, pay attention to me," Brenna said, grinning up at me.

I kissed her softly. "Yes?"

"Paige is fine. She's hanging out with her boyfriend. Stop growling."

"Fine, I'll try. I can't help it. She's my baby sister."

"And your baby sister can take care of herself," Lee said from my other side, and I looked over at my friend.

"It is true, but I can't help it. We're going to get growly about her. It's what we do."

Lee sighed. "On that note, I'm going to go and get

another drink. The commitment vibes are so strong here, it's getting hard to breathe."

I rolled my eyes as Lee walked away, and then I pulled Brenna closer.

"Did you ever think we'd be here?"

"Honestly, last month I didn't think we'd be here, and here we are, heading into our second trimester, and you are about to be a daddy two times over."

I snorted, knowing that while I wasn't going to be called daddy, yes, my genes were about to make two people.

This wasn't how I expected my future to be, but it was better than anything I could ever have wanted.

I held Brenna close, kissed her again, and ignored the laughter and warmth and everything else around us.

The Montgomerys would always be there, but for this moment, I just needed Brenna.

The woman I never expected, the friend I had always hidden away from myself.

And my other half.

And the woman I would be forever devoted to, to the end of my days.

RESOLUTION

Paige

Tonight was the night.

After over a year of dating, tonight was the night Colton and I would finally take the next step. He'd called me this morning and asked me to meet him at one of our favorite spots. He'd sounded so nervous and told me that he was excited over something. Colton had sent over flowers the day before with a note saying, 'just because' and I couldn't stop smiling.

Tonight, Colton would get down on one knee and propose to me. And I would say yes.

I loved him with every ounce of my soul and could not wait until we started our life together.

I bit my lip as I looked into the mirror, pinning my

hair back from my face. I loved Colton. He made me smile, made me laugh, and I knew I'd spend the rest of my life with him. He was my everything, and I could not wait to say yes.

I wore a light peach wrap-dress, one that I loved and made me happy to wear. I felt pretty and like a princess. Instead of a crown, I had a planner and a tablet, but it worked for me. Just in case tonight *wasn't* the night, I still looked and felt pretty. I was a realist with my head in the clouds for only moments, not the entire day, after all.

With one last look in the mirror, I made my way to my car, singing and dancing in my seat as I drove toward the park. The night was beautiful, with not a cloud in sight. The moon was full, and the sky was bright.

Romance filled the air, and if I were any more jovial and lighthearted, I'd be filled with cotton candy and annoy the hell out of my family.

I smirked as I parked, shaking my head. I was the giddy one of the group, just like Archer, but I probably hit the annoyance factor more. I didn't mind since a grumpy Montgomery was a normal Montgomery. I'd be the weird one.

Hopefully, later tonight, I'd be the *engaged* weird one.

I picked up my bag and did my best not to skip to our meeting spot on the patio outside of Colton's restaurant in the park. We'd met at this spot, and I'd fallen for him at that exact moment.

Montgomerys didn't always fall at first sight, but when they did, it lasted.

I gripped my hands tightly in front of me as Colton came forward, his blond hair messy and pushed back from his face. The ends reached his collar, and while I knew he wanted a haircut, I liked the surfer look on him. He was gorgeous, tan, intelligent, caring, and *mine*.

"Paige."

His voice was smooth whiskey that slid over me, and I couldn't help but smile wide. I loved this man so much, and it almost hurt sometimes because it was too much. I'd never fallen like this before, and I wasn't sure how I was supposed to make clear and coherent thoughts when he was around.

"Colton." I went up to my tiptoes and pressed my lips to his. He was taller than me, so he always had to lean down for me to kiss him. I didn't mind. He always made sure I could have his lips, his taste—his everything.

"I'm glad you could make it. I have a busy shift

tonight but wanted to talk with you about something important and time-sensitive."

I blinked, wondering if this was a different way to begin a proposal. I'd never been proposed to, however, so I wasn't sure.

"I'm here. Thank you so much for inviting me out tonight. I love this spot. It's the first place I met you." My heart raced, and I told myself to calm down.

He blinked, distracted. "That's right. I forgot. I like it because it's so close to the restaurant, so I don't have to take much time away. You know?"

Not really, but maybe I was making too much of his words.

"I'm glad it's close, then."

He smiled. "I have great news, Paige. Do you know Massimo? The chef out in New York that's opening a new place?"

I tilted my head, dread pooling in my belly as my dreams of the evening began to shatter like fine glass all around me. "I remember him."

He'd been a jerk and an egotistical asshole when he'd visited and had treated Colton like something under his shoe, but I didn't mention that part.

"Good! Because he offered me a position. Head fucking chef. He needs someone to do it all. As a *partner*. It won't just be his place, but *ours*. I'll get to work with one of the best, Paige. It's been a dream of mine since I was a kid to own a restaurant in New York and be in the *scene*, and now I finally get my chance. I'm so fucking excited, babe."

I swallowed hard, the ringing in my head growing louder as I tried to keep up. "New York? As in... not in Colorado? What... what are you talking about, Colton?"

He seemed to realize he might have said the wrong thing because he winced before reaching out to cup my face. I took a step back, not sure I wanted him to touch me at that moment. I wasn't sure what I'd say to him if he did.

"Babe."

"Please don't call me babe." I'd never hated it before, but I didn't like it then.

"Paige. This is a great opportunity. Once in a lifetime."

"I thought *we* were once in a lifetime."

He grimaced. "Paige, baby. It's a huge chance—my big break. I mean... I guess you can come with me."

He *guessed*. As in, he wasn't sure. As in, I wasn't at the forefront of his mind.

"My entire family is here, Colton. My job. My life. I can't just move to New York and start another Montgomery Builders. That's not how this works."

He ran his hand through his hair. "Shit. I didn't think you'd react like this."

"How am I supposed to react, Colton? I thought you were going to fucking propose, and now you're saying you're moving across the country and didn't think about what would happen to me when you did?" I hadn't meant to let all of those words out, and now there was no way to take them back.

Colton blanched. "Paige...it's not that I don't like you. I do."

I held up my hand before he could break my heart any more than he had. "Don't. Don't placate me. Clearly, we were looking at this relationship from very different places. I—I can't look at you right now." I didn't want him to see me break.

"I need to head back, Paige. I can't let them do this without me. We'll talk later. I promise. We'll figure something out."

I met his gaze, grateful that my eyes were dry. "No, don't. It's fine. Go. Just go."

Then he did the only thing he could do, the only thing that broke me. He left. And he didn't look back.

I stood on our spot, grateful for the privacy, but I couldn't breathe. I couldn't think.

I'd thought I'd found my happiness. I thought I was ready for my future.

It turned out I was once again the baby Montgomery with her head in the clouds and stars in her eyes. Colton didn't love me. Colton wasn't my forever. And somehow, I was supposed to walk away from here as if nothing had happened.

My body began to shake, and I pulled out my phone, knowing I needed someone. I couldn't breathe. I couldn't drive. I needed help.

Only I didn't want to put that on their shoulders. I didn't want to bother them and have them worry about little Paige again. That's all they'd done my entire life.

I rolled my shoulders back and made my way to my car. I'd deal with this alone—just like I should have done in the beginning.

I'd put my faith in the wrong man, and I promised myself I'd never do it again.

The Montgomerys fell hard, and now it seemed they broke even harder.

I'd fallen once, and I vowed to myself even as I fought through the pain, I'd never do it again.

I'd never fall in love with anyone ever again.

No matter what fate tossed my way.

Next in the Montgomery Ink series?
Paige and... Lee change everything in Inked Craving

WANT TO READ A SPECIAL BONUS EPILOGUE FEATURING BENJAMIN & BRENNA CLICK HERE!

A NOTE FROM CARRIE ANN RYAN

Thank you so much for reading **INKED DEVOTION!**

This book was honestly a blast to write. I loved the fact that not only did Brenna surprise me, but Benjamin's story did as well. I loved how they twisted together and how these Montgomerys are tugging on my heart!

Next up in the Montgomery Ink series?

Paige and Lee change the game. Yes. I said Paige and Lee. Inked Craving will break my heart and I honestly cannot wait.

The Montgomery Ink: Fort Collins Series:

Book 1: Inked Persuasion

Book 2: Inked Obsession

Book 3: Inked Devotion

Book 3.5: Nothing But Ink

Book 4: Inked Craving

Book 5: Inked Temptation

If you want to make sure you know what's coming next from me, you can sign up for my newsletter at www. CarrieAnnRyan.com; follow me on twitter at @Carrie-AnnRyan, or like my Facebook page. I also have a Facebook Fan Club where we have trivia, chats, and other goodies. You guys are the reason I get to do what I do and I thank you.

Make sure you're signed up for my MAILING LIST so you can know when the next releases are available as well as find giveaways and FREE READS.

Happy Reading!

WANT TO READ A SPECIAL **BONUS EPILOGUE** FEATURING BENJAMIN **&** BRENNA **CLICK HERE!**

ALSO FROM CARRIE ANN RYAN

The Montgomery Ink Legacy Series:

Book 1: Bittersweet Promises (Leif & Brooke)

Book 2: At First Meet (Nick & Lake)

Book 2.5: Happily Ever Never (May & Leo)

Book 3: Longtime Crush (Sebastian & Raven)

Book 4: Best Friend Temptation (Noah, Ford, and Greer)

Book 4.5: Happily Ever Maybe (Jennifer & Gus)

Book 5: Last First Kiss (Daisy & Hugh)

Book 6: His Second Chance (Kane & Phoebe)

Book 7: One Night with You (Kingston & Claire)

Book 8: Accidentally Forever (Crew & Aria)

Book 9: Last Chance Seduction (Lexington & Mercy)

Book 10: Kiss Me Forever (Brooklyn & Reece)

Book 11: His Guilty Pleasure (Dash & Aly)

Book 12: Maybe it's You (Riley & Gage)

The Cage Family

Book 1: The Forever Rule (Aston & Blakely)

Book 2: An Unexpected Everything (Isabella & Weston)

Book 3: If You Were Mine (Dorian & Harper)

Book 4: One Quick Obsession (Hudson & Scarlett)

Book 5: Pretend it's Forever (Sophia & Carson)

Book 6: Wish it Were You (Flynn & Luna)

Ashford Creek

Book 1: Legacy (Callum & Felicity)

Book 2: Crossroads (Bodhi & Kiera)

Book 3: Westward (Atlas & Elizabeth)

Book 4: Patience (Teagan & Rush)

Clover Lake

Book 1: Always a Fake Bridesmaid (Livvy & Ewan)

Book 2: Accidental Runaway Groom (Jamie & Sharp)

Book 3: His Practically Fake Proposal (Galen & Addy)

The Wilder Brothers Series:

Book 1: One Way Back to Me (Eli & Alexis)

Book 2: Always the One for Me (Evan & Kendall)

Book 3: The Path to You (Everett & Bethany)

Book 4: Coming Home for Us (Elijah & Maddie)

Book 5: Stay Here With Me (East & Lark)

Book 6: Finding the Road to Us (Elliot, Trace, and Sidney)

Book 7: Moments for You (Ridge & Aurora)

Book 7.5: A Wilder Wedding (Amos & Naomi)

Book 8: Forever For Us (Wyatt & Ava)

Book 9: Pieces of Me (Gabriel & Briar)

Book 10: Endlessly Yours (Brooks & Rory)

The Falling for the Cassidy Brothers Series:

(Formerly the First Time Series)

Book 1: Good Time Boyfriend (Heath & Devney)

Book 2: Last Minute Fiancé (Luca & Addison)

Book 3: Second Chance Husband (August & Paisley)

Montgomery Ink Denver:

Book 0.5: Ink Inspired (Shep & Shea)

Book 0.6: Ink Reunited (Sassy, Rare, and Ian)

Book 1: Delicate Ink (Austin & Sierra)

Book 1.5: Forever Ink (Callie & Morgan)

Book 2: Tempting Boundaries (Decker and Miranda)

Book 3: Harder than Words (Meghan & Luc)

Book 3.5: Finally Found You (Mason & Presley)

Book 4: Written in Ink (Griffin & Autumn)

Book 4.5: Hidden Ink (Hailey & Sloane)

Book 5: Ink Enduring (Maya, Jake, and Border)

Book 6: Ink Exposed (Alex & Tabby)

Book 6.5: Adoring Ink (Holly & Brody)

Book 6.6: Love, Honor, & Ink (Arianna & Harper)

Book 7: Inked Expressions (Storm & Everly)

Book 7.3: Dropout (Grayson & Kate)

Book 7.5: Executive Ink (Jax & Ashlynn)

Book 8: Inked Memories (Wes & Jillian)

Book 8.5: Inked Nights (Derek & Olivia)

Book 8.7: Second Chance Ink (Brandon & Lauren)

Book 8.5: Montgomery Midnight Kisses (Alex & Tabby Bonus(

Bonus: Inked Kingdom (Stone & Sarina)

Montgomery Ink: Colorado Springs

Book 1: Fallen Ink (Adrienne & Mace)

Book 2: Restless Ink (Thea & Dimitri)

Book 2.5: Ashes to Ink (Abby & Ryan)

Book 3: Jagged Ink (Roxie & Carter)

Book 3.5: Ink by Numbers (Landon & Kaylee)

The Montgomery Ink: Boulder Series:

Book 1: Wrapped in Ink (Liam & Arden)

Book 2: Sated in Ink (Ethan, Lincoln, and Holland)

Book 3: Embraced in Ink (Bristol & Marcus)

Book 3: Moments in Ink (Zia & Meredith)

Book 4: Seduced in Ink (Aaron & Madison)

Book 4.5: Captured in Ink (Julia, Ronin, & Kincaid)

Book 4.7: Inked Fantasy (Secret ??)

Book 4.8: A Very Montgomery Christmas (The Entire Boulder Family)

The Montgomery Ink: Fort Collins Series:

Book 1: Inked Persuasion (Jacob & Annabelle)

Book 2: Inked Obsession (Beckett & Eliza)

Book 3: Inked Devotion (Benjamin & Brenna)

Book 3.5: Nothing But Ink (Clay & Riggs)

Book 4: Inked Craving (Lee & Paige)

Book 5: Inked Temptation (Archer & Killian)

The Promise Me Series:

Book 1: Forever Only Once (Cross & Hazel)

Book 2: From That Moment (Prior & Paris)

Book 3: Far From Destined (Macon & Dakota)

Book 4: From Our First (Nate & Myra)

The Whiskey and Lies Series:

Book 1: Whiskey Secrets (Dare & Kenzie)

Book 2: Whiskey Reveals (Fox & Melody)

Book 3: <u>Whiskey Undone</u> (Loch & Ainsley)

The Gallagher Brothers Series:
Book 1: <u>Love Restored</u> (Graham & Blake)
Book 2: <u>Passion Restored</u> (Owen & Liz)
Book 3: <u>Hope Restored</u> (Murphy & Tessa)

The Carr Family Series:
(Formerly the Less Than Series)
Book 1: Breathless With Her (Devin & Erin)
Book 2: Reckless With You (Tucker & Amelia)
Book 3: Shameless With Him (Caleb & Zoey)

The Fractured Connections Series:
Book 1: Breaking Without You (Cameron & Violet)
Book 2: Shouldn't Have You (Brendon & Harmony)
Book 3: Falling With You (Aiden & Sienna)
Book 4: Taken With You (Beckham & Meadow)

The Campus Roommates Series:
(Formerly the On My Own Series)
Book 0.5: My First Glance
Book 1: My One Night (Dillon & Elise)
Book 2: My Rebound (Pacey & Mackenzie)
Book 3: My Next Play (Miles & Nessa)
Book 4: My Bad Decisions (Tanner & Natalie)

The Ravenwood Coven Series:

Book 1: Dawn Unearthed

Book 2: Dusk Unveiled

Book 3: Evernight Unleashed

The Aspen Pack Series:

Book 1: Etched in Honor

Book 2: Hunted in Darkness

Book 3: Mated in Chaos

Book 4: Harbored in Silence

Book 5: Marked in Flames

The Talon Pack:

Book 1: Tattered Loyalties

Book 2: An Alpha's Choice

Book 3: Mated in Mist

Book 4: Wolf Betrayed

Book 5: Fractured Silence

Book 6: Destiny Disgraced

Book 7: Eternal Mourning

Book 8: Strength Enduring

Book 9: Forever Broken

Book 10: Mated in Darkness

Book 11: Fated in Winter

Redwood Pack Series:

Book 0.5: <u>An Alpha's Path</u>

Book 1: <u>A Taste for a Mate</u>

Book 2: <u>Trinity Bound</u>

Book 2.5: <u>A Night Away</u>

Book 3: <u>Enforcer's Redemption</u>

Book 3.5: <u>Blurred Expectations</u>

Book 3.7: <u>Forgiveness</u>

Book 4: <u>Shattered Emotions</u>

Book 5: <u>Hidden Destiny</u>

Book 5.5: <u>A Beta's Haven</u>

Book 6: <u>Fighting Fate</u>

Book 6.5: <u>Loving the Omega</u>

Book 6.7: <u>The Hunted Heart</u>

Book 7: <u>Wicked Wolf</u>

The Elements of Five Series:

Book 1: From Breath and Ruin

Book 2: From Flame and Ash

Book 3: From Spirit and Binding

Book 4: From Shadow and Silence

Dante's Circle Series:

Book 1: <u>Dust of My Wings</u>

Book 2: <u>Her Warriors' Three Wishes</u>

Book 3: <u>An Unlucky Moon</u>

Book 3.5: <u>His Choice</u>

Book 4: <u>Tangled Innocence</u>
Book 5: <u>Fierce Enchantment</u>
Book 6: <u>An Immortal's Song</u>
Book 7: <u>Prowled Darkness</u>
Book 8: Dante's Circle Reborn

Holiday, Montana Series:
Book 1: <u>Charmed Spirits</u>
Book 2: <u>Santa's Executive</u>
Book 3: <u>Finding Abigail</u>
Book 4: <u>Her Lucky Love</u>
Book 5: Dreams of Ivory

The Branded Pack Series:
(Written with Alexandra Ivy)
Book 1: <u>Stolen and Forgiven</u>
Book 2: <u>Abandoned and Unseen</u>
Book 3: <u>Buried and Shadowed</u>

ABOUT THE AUTHOR

Carrie Ann Ryan is the New York Times and USA Today bestselling author of contemporary, paranormal, and young adult romance. Her works include the Montgomery Ink, Redwood Pack, Fractured Connections, and Elements of Five series, which have sold over 3.0 million books worldwide. She started writing while in graduate school for her advanced degree in chemistry and hasn't stopped since. Carrie Ann has written over seventy-five novels and novellas with more in the works. When she's not losing herself in her emotional and action-packed worlds, she's reading as much as she can while wrangling her clowder of cats who have more followers than she does.

www.CarrieAnnRyan.com

www.ingramcontent.com/pod-product-compliance
Lightning Source LLC
Chambersburg PA
CBHW061011120726
47910CB00006B/1884